A BOATLOAD

(A JACK MCCOUL CAPER BOOK 1)

DWIGHT HOLING

A BOATLOAD

(A Jack McCoul Caper)

Print Edition

Published by Jackdaw Press

This book is a work of fiction. Names, characters, places, and incidents are either products of the author's imagination or are used factiously. Any resemblance to actual persons, living or dead, is entirely coincidental.

The author acknowledges the trademarked status and trademark owners of various products referenced in this work of fiction, which have been used without permission. The publication/use of these trademarks is not authorized, associated with, or sponsored by the trademark owners.

ISBN: 978-0-9911301-2-2

For More Information, please visit dwightholing.com.

See how you can **Get a Free Book** at the end of this novel.

For Annie, Mary & Sam

1

Jack McCoul found Hark waiting behind the wheel of a '64 Impala lowrider that was the color of a Golden Gate sunset. A pair of Locs hid Hark's eyes, the top of the black frames level to the bandana he pulled low on his forehead. Gothic letters blued his wide neck. He got the tat when he belonged to a Mission District gang, but the inker misspelled his name. He started Geraldo with an *H* and forgot the *o* before adding angel wings. It was how Hark got his handle. He was used to it, even his grandma called him that, but Jack never made the mistake of singing the Christmas carol around him. He didn't even hum it.

"Katie said to say hello," Jack said. "She's still hoping you'll take her yoga class. Says every man needs to work on being flexible."

Hark flashed a grin. "Not what the ads say on TV, *vato*. All due respect."

Jack opened the shotgun door and slid into the tuck-'n-roll bucket. The ride was so low he instinctively puckered as they eased away from the curb in front of his loft.

"Where to?" Hark asked.

"The Marina."

"How come? Nothing there but fancy boats and *gabachos* with two hundred dollar haircuts."

"Katie's brother Brad is there polishing yachts, walking the owners' dogs. He ran into a jam."

"Door or strawberry?"

Jack gave him a look. "Seriously?"

Hark shrugged. "Hey, the Giants haven't started playing yet. All I got to watch is old *Loco Comedy Jam* DVDs and George Lopez on the YouTube."

"Brad was playing hold'em with some rollers at a yacht club and started writing paper. They threatened to drop him in the bay so he came crying to Katie. The only way I could keep the peace was to spot him. Now he's late. Not answering my calls. Like his phone fell overboard."

"You know he took your bank to another game and lost it."

"Family. What you going do?"

"You married the sister, not the brother. They're always dead weight. You got to cut him off." He gave it a beat. "Okay, so you cut him a little too. Show him not to disrespect you."

"Why I called you. I need to send an overdraft message to whoever's really between me and my money."

"So that's the way it is? I'm just arm candy?" Hark sighed. "I miss the old days, back when I was what my counselor called a misguided youth."

"Acting out," Jack said. "What you were doing when you were 'banging. That's what the experts would say now."

"And the tour I signed up to do in the 'Stan instead of going to Stockton Correctional? What would your experts call that?"

"Hobson's choice."

"Don't know the dude, but I do know this. Reason I made it out of there alive was what I learned on the streets. The importance of looking out for your *hermanos*. Defending your turf."

"Hooah," Jack said. "Army of one."

They drove to the Embarcadero and followed it north along the gray-green waters. Clouds scudded across the sky. A tug churned beneath the Bay Bridge.

Jack and Katie had a view of it from their place in a live-work building within earshot of the bats cracking at AT&T Park. The loft came with a membership to an exclusive gym on the second floor. Katie led classes there. Step, spinning, Zumba. She was trying to build a private practice. Yoga and Pilates were her specialties.

Jack was all for it. It got him closer to his neighbors, which was the reason he picked the place. They were all young and getting rich from designing apps and games, and Jack, now that he had gone legit, fancied himself a venture capitalist. He was always on the lookout to invest in the next big thing. It wasn't that long ago he would have searched among the earnest techies for the oligarchs who lived for cutting corners in order to enrich themselves at the expense of others. Their egos and stock options made them ripe targets for high-tech variations of the *Nigerian Prince* and other types of cons. Nothing was more rewarding than skinning a fat cat. But those days were over. Jack had promised Katie when they got married he would stay off the grift for good, and except for an occasional slip-up, he kept his word.

"How much is he in to you for?" Hark asked as they pulled up to the light in front of the Ferry Building.

"Fifty."

"Not counting the points."

A kid on a skateboard zipped past on the sidewalk and dodged a couple of tourists dressed in matching cruise ship jackets.

Hark sighed. "You didn't charge points, did you?"

"Katie," Jack said, shrugging.

Hark sighed again and the light changed and he mashed the gas pedal. The twin Flowmasters backfired as the Impala fishtailed off the line.

Jack glanced at the side mirror. "You need to adjust the baffling. Those tourists jumped out of their tennies."

"I'm testing a new manifold," Hark said. "It's what you do when you're a businessman. Servicing my fellow low lows and bombing their rides. I got to know my inventory so I can vouch for it personal."

"A regular Henry Ford, aren't you? Turning the wheels of the American automobile industry."

"Just saying."

Jack pointed at Hark's boiler. "When you're doing all that high finance, you might want to push away from your grandma's table a little more often."

"Hey, you ate her carnitas plenty the nights you used to bail out of your house. Who can say no to seconds?"

Jack nodded. It was true. By the time their senior year at St. Joseph's rolled around, he'd eaten more carne asada and frijoles than corned beef and cabbage. His father was to blame. Gavin would come home jacked up after fighting a fire and start throwing punches, along with empty Guinness bottles.

"Speaking of food, what you think the odds are this fancy yacht club will serve us up some crab Louie?" Hark said.

"About as good as Brad having the money he owes me," Jack said.

~

THE FRANCISCAN YACHT Club was tucked between the sprawling grassy field at Marina Green and the lapping waters of the bay. Its parking lot resembled a Benz and Beamer dealership. The valet's mouth gawped when the lowrider pulled up.

"The driver's going to wait right here," Jack told him. "I won't be long."

"Your driver?" Hark frowned before putting some attitude into it. "Yes, sir, *jefe*. You want me to shine the car while I wait?"

"Katie's brother pulls a Usain Bolt I'll ping you to intercept. You can't miss him. He looks like her."

"Nobody looks like Katie," Hark said. "All due respect."

THE CLUB'S lobby was paneled in redwood and smelled not of old growth forest but of old money. A granite stairway led to a dining room with floor-to-ceiling windows. It was cantilevered over the bay. The view of Alcatraz and the bridge was one in a million. It was unobstructed except when sloops passed by so close their spinnakers filled the glass. A horseshoe-shaped bar ringed by captain's chair stools was tucked in the far corner and partitioned from the members-only restaurant. Jack heard leather cups rattling with liar's dice, the slam of the cups on the polished mahogany, and a chirpy voice making bets. Brad was sitting next to a burly sailor.

"Ahoy," Jack said.

Katie's little brother spun around so fast he knocked over the leather cup and sent the ivory cubes skittering across the shiny bar. Jack clamped a hand on Brad's shoulder. The muscled-up sailor growled and started to rise. He had thick wrists, sun-bleached eyebrows, and a face that was proof he'd never learned how to duck the wind, or a punch.

Jack smiled at him. "Avast, matey. I'm family."

Brad flinched as Jack squeezed harder. "It's true," he said. "He's my sister's, ah,..."

"Husband," Jack said, taking a tone used for little kids and old dogs. "Remember the wedding? Oh, that's right, you missed it. Got stuck in Reno. Something about a casino putting a hold on you after you went over your credit limit and tried squeezing out the men's room window."

"Always the comedian," Brad said with a squeaky laugh.

Jack yanked Brad from the stool. The sailor with the ruddy face started to get up again, but Jack waved him off. "We're going to shiver our timbers."

They walked downstairs and went outside. Hark spotted them and jumped out of the front seat fast for a man his size and stood next to the Impala's trunk. He leveled his Locs on Brad like the bores of a double-barreled 12-gauge.

"What's he doing here?" Brad said.

"Focus," Jack said. "You don't need to worry about Hark. Not yet anyway. You need to worry about the fifty large. About how you're going to give it back. Cash is best. Now is better. We'll give you a lift to the bank."

Jack pushed Brad toward Hark. He made a show of popping the trunk.

Brad tried to dig his topsiders into the asphalt but only managed to scuff them. He searched frantically for the valet. The car jockey had ducked behind a SUV.

"Hold it," Brad said. "Hold it. I'm going to get you the money. I am. Just be patient. This play I'm working? It's going to pay off bigger than Apple. It's not a matter of if, it's when."

"There's no when with me. There's only now." Jack gave him another shove.

Brad threw a Hail Mary. "In a week you'll be kicking yourself ten times over. And that's a lowball. I can't wait to see Katie's face when I tell her you could've turned fifty thou into a half mill—if only you'd seen the bigger picture."

Jack hesitated. He knew plenty about baiting and setting a hook. He'd made a career of it. But the extra zeros were definitely worth a nibble. Ignoring Hark, who was shaking his head and muttering careful, Jack said the word he knew Brad was praying for: "Bullshit."

"It's the real deal. I guarantee it," Brad said, lighting up.

"You got two seconds."

"China," he said. "A boatload."

Hark groaned. "Cups and saucers?"

Jack took a step toward his brother-in-law. "If you're trading humans or heroin, I'll turn you in myself. Katie would kill me if she found out I knew about it and didn't stop you."

Brad smirked. "So old school, bro. Electronics. The new currency. A new generation of microchips. Faster, smaller, and self-healing. Best of all, cheaper. A whole lot cheaper because there's no import duty to pay and plenty of backend."

"Okay, you got my attention," Jack said.

"I've got a shipping container full of them coming in. Do you know how many smart chips the size of a fingernail can fit into a container as big as a boxcar? Once it unloads and I get my cut, I'll pay you back ten to one."

Jack waved him off. "The money isn't in hardware anymore. It's all in software and games and apps and online advertising. Chips aren't worth a dime unless they're in a mobile device people are willing to stand in line for. And since phones and tablets aren't made in the good old US of A, you'll have to send the chips back where they came from."

"That's the beauty," Brad said, preening. "There's an old manufacturing plant down the road. We sneak the chips in and say we made them there. That entitles us to stimulus money from the Feds. Uncle Sam is paying big bucks to beat the Chinese at their own game. There are even laws saying any product sold here has to have a percentage of it manufactured here. Every company selling wireless whatevers will be begging us for the chips. I told you it's a dead bang."

Jack had a thousand questions. Like how Brad got into the

play and why the chips were coming in by ship and not plane, but the main thing he wanted to know was who was behind it. Brad was too much of a wiggler to have thought it up on his own. If Jack was to have any chance of seeing his money again, much less making a profit, there needed to be some brains at the helm.

"Get real," he said. "Nobody would trust you to fetch a bag of potato chips much less smart chips. Who's running the play? What crew?"

Before Brad could answer, the sailor with the sunburned face came storming out. Two guys flanked him. Professional racing-yacht grinders from the look of their bread loaf–sized biceps.

"Hold it right there," the ugly sailor growled. He grabbed hold of Brad's elbow and started to steer him away.

Jack feigned surprise and an accent to go with it. "Why, my good sir, whatever is the meaning of this?"

The sailor pushed Brad toward the twin winch monkeys and faced Jack. "Shove off, asshole. This club's for members only."

Hark was at Jack's side in a flash. He chest bumped the sailor. "*Chingate cabron.* Nobody tells us we don't belong nowhere."

The grinders with the big biceps quickly bookended the sailor, one of them yanking Brad after him. Hark didn't blink.

"Now, now. Everybody take a deep breath," Jack said. "Clearly we have a little misunderstanding."

"No misunderstanding here," Hark said, shifting his weight and balling his fists.

Jack smiled at the trio squaring off with Hark. "You boys go play with your boats. Brad and I can catch up on family time later."

After some snarling and muscle flexing, they led Brad into the yacht club.

Hark shook his head. "I don't get it, '*mano*. How come you let them go?"

"Because of the computer chips," Jack said.

"Come on, you don't believe that punk's got game enough to make that kind of score and pay you back. And that crew? They're not members here, just hired help."

"Exactly. But I see who's holding their leash."

A man was watching from the second floor window. "Who's the Rolex model?" Hark asked.

"Sinclair Huntington."

"The high-tech billionaire who races all those million dollar sailboats?"

"The one and only."

"What makes you think he's behind the chip scam?"

Jack smiled. "Because coincidences are for Scientologists."

2

Hark dropped him off at the loft, and Jack went straight to the second-floor gym. He found Katie leading a step class. Her tank top was the color of a sliced peach, and her black crops were so tight he saw the outline of the tiny mole on her left hip. Several women clutched two-pound, rubber-coated dumbbells and followed her lead as she danced to the beat that blasted from the surround sound. Jack got Katie's attention. She gave him the smile that was the reason why he still put up with her brother. He flashed his fingers to signal how long they had to make their dinner reservation. It was their anniversary and Jack wasn't about to miss it again.

The last time he blew the date he was pulling one last con—he justified—so he could pay for her anniversary present. The mark was a social media start-up founder and the prize was his IPO shares. Jack used a variation of the *Jamaican Switch* and set up a *Big Store* that masqueraded as a private wealth management firm. He played the part of a stock trader who had devised an elaborate, though illicit, scheme for capital gains tax evasion.

The mark fell for it. Jack was pushing the button on the wire transfer that would have sent the IPO shares into his own offshore account when a massive solar flare crashed the internet. It was a one in a billion astronomical kick in the balls and to make matters worse, it happened less than an hour before Jack and Katie's big celebration.

Jack had to use all his acting skills to keep the mark from pulling the plug on the swindle while international trading slowly went back online. After the trade was executed, the mark took off, believing he'd made the deal of a lifetime. But Jack got home too late to celebrate. Katie had tossed the gourmet dinner she cooked down the disposal and was sound asleep after polishing off a bottle of 1999 J. Schram all by her lonesome.

Jack didn't blame Katie for being angry but as she explained later after makeup sex, it was because she felt so guilty letting all that food go to waste. It was all part of who she was—smart, sexy, and sustainability-minded. She graduated pre-med magna cum laude from Berkeley before deciding to forgo knife and chemistry for her own physical-biological approach to health care. She believed in equal doses of yoga, astrology, and stylish outfits. "Look great, feel great" was what she told her workout students and Katie always practiced what she preached.

Jack climbed the stairs to their loft on the top floor. He had two hours before they needed to leave for dinner. That gave him plenty of time to enjoy a cocktail and the view of San Francisco Bay. A cargo ship passing beneath the Bay Bridge turned his thoughts to Brad's supposed big score. Sinclair Huntington had to be up to his hair gel in the scam. The computer chips were being brought in by sea rather than air because it was a whole lot easier to smuggle contraband on a freighter the size of three football fields than a 747. Since it was only one container, it must be a test run. If the system worked, more would follow. How

Huntington got his hands on the chips didn't matter. He either made them at an offshore fab plant or was bringing in counterfeits.

Jack didn't spend time wondering why Huntington was willing to take such a big risk, even though the vulture capitalist's companies took in more money in a day than most countries did in a year. Jack had met plenty of people like him before —big men with big egos who believed they were bigger and better than everybody else. They all had one thing in common: greed. Dangle what they perceived to be an easy opportunity for making a fast buck regardless of the law and they'd never fail to jump at the chance.

Jack sipped his cocktail. If only he were still on the grift. What he wouldn't give to take on a whale like Huntington and beat him at his own game. It would be the score of all scores. Huntington's reputation for winning at all costs in both business and sailing was legendary. But one thing about people like Huntington: the bigger they were, the harder they fell.

Across the water the lights were coming on over the docks in Oakland. They illuminated the container cranes that had inspired the *Star Wars* walkers. Freighters were lining up to unload. Jack raised his glass and toasted what could be but wouldn't be. He had given his word, and no matter how tempting the prize, he wasn't about to backslide.

~

THE INDIAN RESTAURANT Jack picked for their anniversary dinner was on Potrero Hill. The restaurant had been open a couple of weeks but the Yelps about its magical mix of spices, sauces, and locally grown organic fare had already gone viral.

"The first guy who invents a Tweet you can eat will be a

billionaire," Jack told Katie as they bypassed the line of bro-grammers and hipsters waiting to get in.

Jack wasn't worried about getting a table. He'd done the owner, Sanjay, a favor awhile back. Sanjay's son had developed a killer app but a group of Stanford Business School frat boys tried to pull a *Winklevoss* on him. They nearly got away with it until Hark and Jack paid them a visit. Sanjay beamed when Jack and Katie came through the front door. He clasped his hands in front of his heart and bowed.

Katie, who had shimmied into a sizzling red sari for the occasion, returned the greeting. "*Namaste*," she said.

"You're just like Indian food, babe," Jack said as they took their seats at a prime corner table. "Chili pepper and cardamom in one bite, cinnamon and rose syrup the next."

That earned him a quick kiss, and they ordered several small plates and started washing the alternating flavors down with gulps of icy Kingfisher lager. After the main course Sanjay sent bowls of kulfi and kheer on the house. The ice cream was stirred with chunks of fresh mango and the rice pudding sprinkled with powdered cashews. As Katie spooned up both desserts, Jack sat back and admired her appetite and skintight sari, wondering how he got to be so damn lucky.

They grew up in San Francisco but met in Kathmandu. Jack was there with Bobby Ballena, an old running buddy, for a meet with an antiquities trafficker who chain-smoked Kents and dressed like a North Korean dictator. Jack and Bobby were killing time in a teahouse when Katie and her best friend walked in with a group of New Age types. They were on some kind of spiritual quest led by a pudgy phony out of Marin County. Bobby decided to cut the two women from the herd. He told them he and Jack were on a pilgrimage to get in touch with their souls from a previous life when they were humpback whales. It was like sprinkling fish food on a koi pond.

Soon the four were sitting cross-legged on handloomed pillows sipping chai. That was when the fat phony tried to reel Katie and her friend back in, reminding them he was holding their passports and return tickets and there were absolutely, positively no refunds. Bobby pulled out a Ghurka knife he'd traded a counterfeit iPhone for and started slicing a mango. Didn't say a word. Didn't need to. The wannabe guru's eyes never left that big, curved silver blade. By the time the mango was finished, Katie's and her friend's passports and tickets were stacked next to the teapot. Bobby gave the pudge another glare and suddenly it was autumn. Blue and pink rupee notes, green benjamins, even a couple of traveler checks—they all came fluttering down. As the tour guide scrambled out the door, Katie and Jack were staring into each other's eyes. They hadn't stopped staring since.

The busboy was clearing the table when Jack's phone vibrated. He knew better than to answer when they were on a date, so he let it roll to voice mail. Five seconds later Adele started belting from Katie's clutch and she grabbed it before the next refrain. Wailing poured from the phone louder than "Set Fire to the Rain."

Jack didn't have to guess who it was. "Brad," he said.

Katie frowned, her eyes growing wide despite the eyeliner she'd put on to look like a *rani*. "He's been in some kind of accident," she said.

"So tell him to call triple A."

"He's hurt. We have to get him."

Jack tried one more time, though he knew it was hopeless. "But it's our anniversary."

"We have to." She dragged it out longer than a Hindu prayer.

"You mean *I have to*," he muttered. Jack took the phone and listened. He ordered Brad to stay put.

"We better hurry," Katie said, pushing away from the table.

Jack gave her the keys to the Prius. "Go on home. Hark can give me a lift. We'll pick up Brad, give him a glass of warm milk, and tuck him into bed."

Katie thought it over before blowing him a kiss. "You're the best, but make sure it's soy, okay? Brad's lactose intolerant."

3

By the time Jack paid the bill and congratulated Sanjay on his new eatery, Hark was pulling up.

"*Que paso*?" Hark asked.

"They didn't break his legs, but I got a feeling Brad's not going to be eating solids for a while."

"Where's he bleeding?"

"All over, the way he's whining."

"Hey, remind me to laugh. What sidewalk we got to scrape him off?"

"Waverly Place."

"Chinatown? Don't tell me he's been playing *pai gow* at Fang's."

Hark got the lowrider rolling fast, the hydraulics lifting the body off the chassis so the ass end wouldn't spark every time they hit the dips.

"You and Katie ever have kids, you better hope the brother was adopted. You don't want none of yours catching the dumb gene." Hark palmed the chromed chain link steering wheel. "All due respect."

They crossed under the jade tiles of the Dragon Gate and

followed Grant. "Pull in front and I'll go get him," Jack said. "You better leave the engine running."

"Better I park it and we go in together. You know this place is a triad crib." Hark pulled a Beretta M9 from beneath his bucket and pointed toward the glove box. "I got an extra piece in there since you don't like to carry, especially on a night when you got your hands full with red roses and chocolates."

Hark was right about Jack not being big on shooting irons. If it got to that, then he'd worked it wrong from the get-go.

"A regular boy scout, aren't you?" Jack said.

"It's like Father Bernardus used to tell us at Saint Joe's. 'Be ready to defend yourself.' "

"That was in confirmation class and he was talking about Satan and temptation."

"That too. Why I still keep an AR in the trunk. The old days being not so old."

"Leave them. If it comes to that, Katie'll never speak to me for messing up our anniversary again."

Fang's didn't bother to hide behind a dim sum menu. The two guys standing on either side of the red front door were as implacable as a pair of bronze guardian Fu dog-lions. "Hello, Odd. Evening, Job," Jack said, squeezing between them.

Fang hadn't gotten the memo about rebates for compact fluorescents and no smoking in bars. The place was so dark and smoky that Jack nearly ran smack into Brad, who was hanging upside down from a chain. Brad's eyes darted like a school of fish and a strip of duct tape held in his screams. Six punks dressed in skinny black jeans and tight black T-shirts stood behind him holding automatics. Jack ignored them as he focused on the two men sitting at a gilt-edged, lacquered tea table. A bottle of Johnnie Walker Gold and a carton of Double Happiness were between them. Fang was smoking, the pall rising from both nostrils the same color as his brush cut. His son

Jimmie sat next to him. Word was when Jimmie took his Pearl 60 for a cruise on the bay the sharks trailed him like Pavlov's dogs. He had a thing for Prada shoes, a different pair for every occasion.

Jimmie eyed Jack's leather coat and 501s. "You dress like you work at Google," he said, grimacing. "My tailor will fix you up. Fit you in a nice charcoal suit made of finest British wool with buffalo horn buttons. A Luigi Borrelli tie. You'll look good in an open coffin. I'll tell my boys not to shoot you in the face. My gift to Katie."

"Hello, Jimmie. Sweet of you to remember it's my anniversary."

Jack first met Jimmie when he'd ditched St. Joseph's and took the bus across town to buy firecrackers in Chinatown so he could resell them to the kids back in the Mission. From the beginning it was obvious there was no line Jimmie wouldn't cross, no guilt he'd ever feel. Over the years, Jack and Jimmie had crossed paths and swords doing what they did. Jimmie always kept his eye on the money, while Jack always kept his eye on Jimmie.

Fang didn't say a word. Just kept smoking. Despite his son's bluster, he still called the shots so Jack bowed as a sign of respect and directed his request to him.

"I don't know what Brad owes you but he's in to me for fifty large. I'd say go ahead and let Junior here feed him to his fish friends, but then I'd be out mine and you'd be out yours. My advice? We put him on the street and keep charging him the points. He doesn't make good in a week, I'll load him onto Jimmie's boat myself."

When Jimmie started to protest, his dad waved him off with a cigarette and spoke in Cantonese even though he was San Francisco born and bred. Jack figured the old man did so out of habit; it was the way the triads used to get around bugs planted by the feds before equal opportunity employment laws.

Jimmie translated. "Fang says, your brother's unlucky. He says, give him a paddle and Ping-Pong ball and he'd bet you he could break par at Pebble. Fang says, he's dumb as duck."

"In-law. Brother. In. Law." Jack grinned at Fang. "How about it? Hark and I'll take Brad off your hands. Baby-sit him while he pays off his paper."

The old man said something else. Jimmie translated again. "Fang says, no deal. You find what belongs to us. We'll hold on to your brother. When we get it back, we let him go. Simple."

"What part of *in-law* don't you get?" Jack thought of Katie, thought of what she'd say if he came home empty-handed. "Just for the sake of argument, how much does he owe you?"

Fang's craggy face was lost behind a mushroom cloud of tar and nicotine. Jimmie's smile widened, showing off more teeth than the great whites that trailed his yacht. "Not money," he said. "Integrated circuit microchips. He's part of a crew that ripped off our silicon wafer fab plant in Shenzhen."

Hark whistled. "*Chingame*."

Jack sucked in air and then blew it out. Never could tell which way the fates would blow. San Francisco triads had been running counterfeit software and DVDs that were supplied from their counterparts on the Chinese mainland for years. But manufacturing their own semiconductors? Maybe Fang and son were trying to go legit too.

He looked at the father and then at Jimmie. "To paraphrase your old man, Brad's mental as a mallard. Last year he bought a dozen ferrets off the Internet, pumped them full of steroids, and tried to sell them as toy poodles. You can still find them running around Golden Gate Park." Jack laughed. "Part of an international heist? Brad couldn't handle stealing a purse from a blind lady."

Jimmie pulled on the lapels of his designer suit coat to straighten the drape. "Maybe, but he came here and asked for a seat in our high rollers game. Ante's a G. No limits, no whining. He said he could put up shares in a chip heist as collateral. Like it's some kind of IPO."

Jack pointed toward the unluckiest door knocker in the world. "If Brad knew where your chips were, he'd have told you already. You don't need to do anything more than wave a water glass in front of him, much less soak a towel and strap him to a board."

"Tell me about it. He fainted so many times we put him on the hanger so he'd stop hitting his head. Soiled himself too. Why he's bare-ass naked."

Hark groaned. "I ain't putting him in my ride."

Jack was running out of options. "I'll be straight with you. Same as when I was still in the game. Remember the time I waved you off from dealing with that Russian moneylender because I found out the feds had him under surveillance? Brad mentioned the chips to me this afternoon when I was discussing his repayment plan, but I didn't believe him for a second. He lives in a world they can't draw in comic books. I don't see how I can help you."

The old man coughed, lit one Double Happiness off the other, and said something to his son. Jimmie nodded. "Fang says, you're wasting our time and wasting yours. You want to save your brother? Go find our chips. You tell us where they are, we'll go collect them."

Jack thumped his chest. "I'm honored Fang Family Enterprise thinks so highly of my abilities, but I've been off the streets for too long. I wouldn't know where to start." He pointed at the six gunmen standing behind Brad. "Besides, you got a lot of horsepower. You'll be able to locate them faster than I could."

Jimmie tented his fingers. His nails were long, one pinky nail painted purple. "It's a business decision. You'll do it for free, whereas if we have to do it, there are costs. Triads. It's like a union now. Seniority. Work rules. Mandatory benefits and overtime. The overhead is eating us alive." He smiled menacingly; his teeth gleamed in the darkened room.

Fang hawked up a wad of phlegm and locked his gaze on Jack's. "You are being very slow-witted, Mr. McCoul," he said in English. "This is a most uncomplicated transaction. Locate the chips in exchange for your brother. What part of the terms don't you understand?"

He didn't need to spell out the *or else*. Jack knew arguing was pointless, especially with six guns pointing his way. He crossed the room and squatted so he was level to Brad's face. "I don't care if they hang you in a butcher shop window along with the rest of the plucked ducks, but it's my anniversary and I'm not going to spoil your sister's night. No way, no how." He ripped off the duct tape.

Brad screamed. "Ouch, that really hurt. Why are you being so mean? Get me out of here."

"In a minute. The chips are still on a boat, right?"

"As far as I know."

"So what were you thinking coming in here and trying to gamble with them?"

"Why shouldn't I? I was going to get paid, wasn't I? I was using them like the stock options all the techies get. Those guys get hot cars and hot chicks by showing a piece of paper. What about me? Why shouldn't I be able to do that?"

Jack huffed. "Sinclair Huntington's calling the shots, isn't he? Tell me how he's going to play it. Either I help you or the Fangs use you for a kung fu punching dummy."

Brad started whining. "I don't know anything, I swear. I've never even talked to Mr. Huntington. Only Cutler."

"Who's Cutler?"

"The guy I was playing liar's dice with."

"The sailor with the ruddy face?"

Brad nodded.

"Why did they let you in on the score in the first place?"

"They needed help and I needed money. I told you when I borrowed the fifty thousand from you. I went all in on a dead-bang hand at the yacht club's annual poker world series. Two pairs, cowboys over queens. The other guy draws a quad of deuces. What are the odds? I had to pay it back."

"So Ruddy Face, er, Cutler signs you up as part of the crew to help off-load the chips," Jack said, nodding. "Okay, tell me more about the chips. How are they getting here?"

"All I know is they're in a container on a ship somewhere."

"And it's just a single container?"

"So far."

"You mean, if it gets through more will follow."

"I don't know. They don't tell me anything."

"What did you say to Jimmie?"

"Everything. I had to. Look at what he did to me."

"What's everything?"

"That the chips are in a shipping container. But I don't know on what boat. I don't even know where it is or when it's going to dock or where the old manufacturing plant is."

"But you told Jimmie you're working with a crew who works for Sinclair Huntington."

Brad managed an upside-down nod. "Don't leave me here. Please. Whatever you do, don't leave me. Ask Jimmie to trade me for your fat friend. You got to. I'll die here. Katie will never forgive you. Do it for her."

As much as Jack hated to admit it, the punk was right. If he couldn't pinpoint the whereabouts of the chips, a lot more was at stake than missing an anniversary. When it came to matters of the heart, Katie usually depended on which planet was in which house and which sign was made up of which stars. But there was one area where she didn't bothered to check the zodiac. Brad was the black hole of no-account little brothers, sucking in everyone. Especially Katie. Jack didn't have a choice but to try to restore gravity to its proper balance.

Jack slapped the tape over Brad's mouth and walked to the lacquered tea table. He filled four jade-colored porcelain cups with the JW Gold.

"Deal," he said. "I'll find your chips. In the meantime, don't kill Brad. At least not yet."

4

When Jack got home Katie had the loft aglow in candlelight and net radio tuned to essential jazz. Coltrane was blowing "My Favorite Things" with McCoy Tyner backing him on the ivories. Jack went straight to the fridge for the bottle of J. Schram he'd stashed earlier. He kicked off his shoes and debated stripping off the rest of his clothes to make his grand entrance into the bedroom. In the end he decided to go with the tried and true approach, knowing there was a big difference between anticipation and expectation when it came to romance.

Jack hoped a gibbous moon was shining through the window. Not only because the word *gibbous* sounded so cool, but because Katie always looked good in the moonlight. He was out of luck. Fog thicker than a fleece jacket wrapped the building. The only sign of Katie beneath a down comforter and afghan was a soft purr coming from the middle of the bed. He checked his watch. It was long past midnight. For the second time in a row he'd blown their anniversary.

Jack set the champagne on the nightstand, finished undressing, and slipped under the comforter. Katie's snores didn't miss a beat as he pulled her close. It wasn't exactly the celebration he had in mind, but there was no place he'd rather be than in bed with the woman he loved in the city where he belonged. There was a time when he ran from San Francisco and traveled to wherever a hot credit card took him. But no matter how far and fast Jack ran, San Francisco always called him home. In the end, no other place gave him the feeling he got when he walked its streets, no other made him feel more alive.

His mentor Henri LeConte, an old-school art forger who taught him the way of the grift, showed him how to view the city —a living masterpiece, a never-ending, ever-changing diorama of life. Every generation and all the different cultures added layers to the richness of the bustling canvas. San Francisco was deep under his skin, and it was as much a part of Jack McCoul as he was of it.

Katie was like that too—a part of him and under his skin. Having conned himself into believing she would be okay with it, Jack told her early on in their relationship what he did for a living. At first she moaned as if she were going to be sick, but then she narrowed her eyes as her face reddened with anger. "Am I some kind of mark to you?" She pushed him away hard. "Have you been using me this whole time in some kind of twisted game?"

"No way. I'd never lie to you."

Katie started to calm down after exacting his promise that he would get out of the life, so he tried to return things to normal by joking that he never would have guessed she had such a quick temper. "What happened to all that Zen and yoga?"

That triggered a flash in her eyes again. "I'm a woman, not a Buddha."

Later, he asked her what it was that made her still love him, knowing what she knew. "Any man can follow the rules," she explained. "But being able to break them without losing your soul? That takes a real man."

There was nothing Jack wouldn't do for Katie. He'd go straight; he'd go to the ends of the earth. He'd even find a boatload of hot computer chips and risk getting caught between a warring triad and a billionaire with a larceny streak, if need be. Whatever it took, he'd do it.

"Happy anniversary," he whispered, hoping it was just loud enough.

"Mmm," she said.

"Sorry I'm late."

"Mmm." She burrowed deeper into the pillow.

"Don't worry about Brad."

"Hmm?"

He stuck to his vow of never lying to her. "I didn't take him home."

"Wha'?" The purring stopped.

"He's going to hang around Chinatown for a while."

"Really?" Her eyelashes fluttered against the pillowcase.

"Really," he said.

Katie propped herself on an elbow. "Everything's okay? Brad wasn't hurt after all?"

"He's walking on air. I checked him out head to toe."

She placed her palm on his chest and traced her fingers over his heart. "You're such a good brother-in-law."

"Don't forget about the good husband part."

"I won't," she said, sliding her hand lower.

Jack smiled and thought, "Who needs a gibbous moon?"

KATIE WOKE first and by the time Jack got to the kitchen to hit the espresso machine, she'd already dressed for work in a black leotard, teal tank, and pink cross-trainers. She planted a kiss on his lips. "Best anniversary ever."

"Does it still count even though it was technically the day after?"

"Over and over again, I'd say." She blew a kiss and was out the door.

Jack fixed himself a double espresso, flipped on NPR, and checked e-mail on his tablet. The news was pretty much the same old same old: some war in one sandbox or another and an endless war of words in Washington. He was barely listening as he scrolled through all the spam that had escaped the filter but glanced up quicker than a meerkat when the anchor mentioned Sinclair Huntington. The reporter announced the technopreneur was slotted to give the keynote at the game developer convention. Rumors swirled that the high-tech highness would use the spotlight to debut a revolutionary new product.

The news gave Jack more kick than the espresso shot. It meant Huntington already had a Whitman's Sampler of the smart chips plugged into devices to wow the gamer crowd. It also meant the ship carrying the container was close. The high-tech market moved faster than next season's processor speed, and Huntington would need to be ready to fulfill orders.

Jack Googled Sinclair Huntington and found hundreds of links reporting on his meteoric rise in the world of high tech, sailing, and San Francisco society and politics. Most photographs showed Huntington at the helm of a racing yacht wearing a white ball cap with his company's logo above the bill. It was a modified Jolly Roger with Huntington's portrait as the skull and dollar signs as the crossed cutlasses.

The gushing profiles described him as the digital age version of Horatio Alger. While he didn't have the education to build a computer or design software, he did have the balls to talk his way into the private offices of venture capitalists. Huntington bought up tech businesses run out of garages and fit them together like a jigsaw puzzle. His personal life was as rich in fodder as his business dealings. He'd been married four times. After Huntington divorced his first wife, she stormed into the company's annual board meeting, accused him of years of abuse, pulled a chrome Sig Sauer out of her purse, and shot herself in the head. His next two divorces didn't end in suicides, but they did cost him hundreds of millions. The current Mrs. Huntington was a stunning beauty from Hong Kong who served as his company's chief operating officer.

News articles about Huntington's drive to win sailing competitions portrayed him as no less cold blooded. He rarely lost but when he did, he immediately fired the entire crew and commissioned a new yacht that would be faster and more technologically advanced. He never named a boat after a wife.

Jack put the gossip columns aside and started searching cargo ship landings. A website displayed animated arrows shaped like ships streaming across a digital image of San Francisco Bay. The arrows were color-coded and pinned to the Automatic Identification System, a computerized geographic information system for vessels. He tapped on one. A pop-up listed the ship's name, last port of call, and destination right down to the mooring and terminal number. He tapped on others. Nearly all were freighters ferrying containers back and forth to Asia.

Tired of letting his fingers do the walking, Jack clicked off the tablet and grabbed his jacket.

5

The fog was gone and the sun was out as Jack walked through his neighborhood—a patchwork of warehouses, loft apartments, and Internet start-ups. Somewhere along the line, rich developers hoping to duplicate New York's SoHo District labeled it SoMa but Jack always referred to it by its original name, South of the Slot. The old sobriquet dated back to San Francisco's early days and referred to the cable cars that once clanged up and down Market Street.

He walked along Brannan, one of the many streets named after San Francisco's Irish settlers. Jack dodged a techie riding a Razor and nearly missed being flattened by a Red Bull–fueled bike messenger as he crossed Embarcadero. Sunlight was sparkling on the bay and the seagulls were circling the best bar and burger joint in the city.

Pier Inn had been around forever. A dilapidated joint built on the end of a dilapidated pier. The inn offered no lodging except the bar's floor for regulars who dropped where they drank. If the city fathers and mothers had their way, the Pier would be demolished to make room for a new home for the Warriors. Jack was against it. Not only because he'd been frequenting the joint ever since his old man took him there for his first beer and shot, but because he'd never been a big fan of professional basketball. For starters, the game was played indoors. What's more, everything leading up to the final seconds of play seemed irrelevant. Since the Giants' yard was nearby, the debate over basketball got argued at the Pier as often as the brewing merits of Anchor Steam.

It was a workday for citizens but it was hard to tell at the Pier. Not one of the outdoor picnic tables was empty and it was hip deep inside with tugboat crews, laptopping lone eagles, gamblers, and a couple of fellow grifters. The sound of grease popping on the griddle was as loud as the denizens shouting their drink orders.

It took two people to handle the tiny bar. Lacey nodded when she saw Jack. "Please say you're here to drown your sorrows because pretty Katie finally wised up and left your sorry, scheming ass."

Jack grinned. Lacey had a full sleeve of tattoos and her hair looked like she just stepped off her Harley. "Sorry to disappoint," he said. "Another happy anniversary in the record books by all accounts."

"Damn." Lacey wrinkled her nose, sending a shiny hoop swinging. "Your usual?"

"Please, and sail it to the end. I need to get a word in with Wonder Boy."

"Don't wear him out. He's still got the Giants season ahead of him."

Lacey poured coffee and Jameson in a thick ceramic mug. She was a true professional and didn't spoil it with sugar and whipping cream. Candy drinks were for sorority girls, hypoglycemics, and tourists. Jack moved to where her co-mixologist was holding forth. Wonder Boy was a statistician extraordinaire. Ask him anything about sports—Mays' lifetime OBP, the strike-to-ball ratio in Cain's perfect game—and he'd spit out the answer faster than a mortgage defaulter uttering excuses. It might take him a few tries to wrestle his sibilants to ground, but he was never wrong.

Sports stats weren't Wonder Boy's only specialty. Earthquake dates and their Richter scale points, rock band tours and their song lineups, the phases of the moon and their corresponding tides—high tides, low tides, ebb tides, flood tides—Wonder Boy knew them all. He was a living, breathing tide chart and Doppler radar machine all rolled into one. With his see all perch behind the bar at Pier 30, nothing on the bay got by him. Especially not something as big and slow as a cargo ship with a deck stacked with containers.

"Fastball coming at you, Wonder," Jack said, picking up the heavy mug. "Giants' pitcher with the highest batting average in a single season."

"S-s-smiling Mickey Welch. Hit .333." His lips pursed. "Trick question. He only had three ABs that s-s-season, his final. Lifetime .224 hitter."

"Can't throw anything past you."

Wonder Boy rinsed a beer glass under the tap, gave it a workout with a bar towel. Jack took a sip. The morning dew of Ireland did little to cool the scalding coffee, much less thin its viscosity.

"You got a better view here than the one percenters do at the Franciscan Yacht Club," Jack said. "Yours is a three bridger."

Wonder Boy kept drying the glass. "Bay Bridge the longest. Four point five miles. Sh-sh-shipping clearance the highest. Two hundred and twenty feet."

Jack leaned forward, beckoned Wonder with his chin. "I need to locate a container coming in from China. It could already be here."

"From which port? China has two thousand. S-s-seven of the world's ten biggest."

"My best guess in Shenzhen."

"Fourth biggest in the world."

"It's got to be off-loaded in Oakland, right?"

Wonder nodded. "You know how many sh-sh-ships arrive every day? How many TEUs?"

"What's a TEU?"

"Twenty–foot equivalent unit. What they call a sh-sh-shipping container."

"Got it. A TEU. How many on a typical freighter?"

"The average carries nine thousand. The largest eighteen thousand. Fifty million TEUs sh-sh-shipped worldwide every year. Ten thousand fall overboard."

"Gives new meaning to a needle in a haystack, I know, but say I can ID the vessel I'm looking for. What I'd need next is a look at the manifest to pinpoint the one container, the TEU I'm after, among the thousands on board. The list of the shippers, the receivers, what's inside, that sort of thing."

"Customs would have it. S-s-so would the sh-sh-ship's captain. But what if the listed contents are a beard?"

"I'm betting it will be, but I'm also hoping it'll be easier to spot than a merkin on a Brazilian."

"Good news is everything's electronic. Each TEU has an identifying s-s-serial sh-sh-shipping container code on it. You'll need a way to hack into the s-s-system."

"Why, that would be illegal," Jack said with a smile. He drained the java plus and placed five bucks on the bar. Digital records were better than paper. Saved trees, not to mention time and money. "And hopefully Brad's life," Jack thought.

~

They were waiting for him in front of his building. Jack should've spotted them sooner but he was picturing Katie back from the gym, peeling off her workout getup as she readied to take a shower.

"I need to talk to you," the ugly sailor named Cutler said through the open passenger window of a black Yukon. "Get in. We'll give you a ride."

"No thanks, Ruddy Face. Mom warned me not to take rides from strangers." Jack kept walking.

"Don't call me that again," Cutler said.

The rear doors of the Yukon swung open and the twin winch winders with their chemically engineered biceps flew out. They grabbed Jack's arms and steered him into the backseat. The driver punched the gas.

"That certainly won't help your mileage any," Jack said.

Cutler twisted around. "You got some mouth."

The grinders took that to mean they should slam their elbows into his ribs.

The driver made a couple of turns and they crossed China Basin over the Lefty O'Doul Bridge and drove down Third Street, past Mission Bay, past the old Bethlehem Steel yard, and through Bayview-Hunters Point. The road curved and the ghost-like hulk of Candlestick filled the windshield.

Jack said, "Hey, Ruddy, if you're taking me out to the ball game you're a little off course. The Giants have been playing downtown since 2000 and the 'Niners moved to Santa Clara."

That earned another round of elbows to the ribs.

Acres of cracked and potholed asphalt surrounded the decrepit stadium. The driver pulled to a stop in the middle of the parking lot but kept the engine running.

Cutler turned sideways again. "Did you ever watch that show where they blew up Texas Stadium? It was something. They start off with a big fireworks show, all the fans watching from behind these barricades, and then the real show begins. A controlled implosion they call it. Boom. Boom. Boom. The whole thing just falls in on itself."

The sailor's grin was lopsided. "They can't do that here because Candlestick's not a dome. They got to take it down like they did the old Yankee Stadium. Bit by bit. They turn these big machines loose that chew it up like termites munching rotten wood. They grind the bleachers and concrete into dust."

Cutler glanced at Candlestick and then faced Jack again. "You know what they say about Yankee Stadium? Every night a body or two got dumped there. In the morning they'd be ground up with everything else. Nothing left to find."

Jack shrugged. "So you watch the History Channel. Good for you. Given your hot and bothered complexion, I figured you for a porn man."

The elbows started up again.

Cutler sneered. "You got a smart mouth, McCoul, but you're not so smart. I think you're dumb like your little brother."

"Brother. In. Law. Why can't you people get that straight?"

"Where is he?"

"Why, is he lost?"

Jack braced for elbows.

"You don't want to play it this way." Cutler made a show of cracking his jaw.

"You got a brother-in-law?" Jack said. "The only time you keep track of them is when your wife invites them for Christmas dinner and they stay til Easter."

Again, the elbows.

Jack worked not to show any pain. "Try real hard. Think about it. I tracked Brad to the Franciscan to get him to pay me what he owed me. Then you stuck your ruddy face in it and led him away before I could collect. He still owes me fifty grand."

Cutler rubbed his pockmarked chin, nibbling on the half

truths. "Tell me where Brad's holed up and there could be a finder's fee in it for you."

"How much?"

"Depends if your information is any good."

"Not a big fan of say now, pay later. Why are you looking for him?"

"That's my business."

"You mean Sinclair Huntington's."

"That's none of your business."

"You don't raise a sail or pull up your pants without Sinclair Huntington telling you to. Why's Huntington care about a punk like Brad?"

"Who says he does? Why, what did Brad tell you?"

"How much is it worth to you?"

Cutler gave a nod to the twin winch winders. "Give it to him."

Left Monkey quickly threw his arm around Jack's neck and locked his elbow, making a fist and tucking it beneath his own chin. The stiff forearm started squeezing off Jack's air. At the same time, Right Monkey started hammering away at Jack's kidneys.

"You're out of your league, McCoul," Cutler said, clearly enjoying the show. "I did some checking. I know all about you. If you think you can hide your brother from me, you're wrong. Wrong will get you hurt. Tell me what he told you."

Jack grabbed Left Monkey's forearm and tried prying it loose from his throat. Red and white lights flashed and a black object hurtled toward him. His ears rang. He pulled harder on the forearm.

Cutler narrowed his eyes to slits. "You got three seconds before you go under." He gestured at Candlestick. "Then we're going haul you out to the fifty yard line and put you in a hole.

They're going build a shopping mall on top of you. Last chance. Where's Brad? What did he tell you?"

Jack tried to pull on the forearm but his fingers stopped responding. It was all he could do to nod.

Cutler told the grinders to ease up. Jack coughed and sucked in air, gulping and gagging as it filled his lungs. Nothing ever tasted sweeter.

Cutler grinned. "You got something you want to say?"

Jack thought about telling him exactly where Brad was hanging, let the ruddy-headed sailor and the twin monkeys take on the Fangs and their six pack of triad shooters but as Jack's old man Gavin used to harp, a job worth doing was a job worth doing yourself. He made some sputtering noises and a pleading roll of the eyes.

Cutler leaned forward. When he did, Jack grabbed the sailor's ears and yanked his head down hard, smashing his sunburned face into the console. Then he dove on top of him and grabbed a fistful of the driver's hair and started slamming his forehead into the steering wheel. He yanked the shift lever and jammed it into drive. The Yukon lurched forward and the big V-8's high idle got the wheels rolling.

The winch monkeys were on Jack in a flash, clawing at his hips and shoulders and trying to pull him off Cutler and the driver. The back bench had plenty of legroom and Jack began mule kicking for all he was worth as the Yukon picked up speed and raced across the empty parking lot.

The SUV smashed head on into a concrete wall and the windshield spidered on impact. There was a bang and a whoosh as the airbags exploded out of the dashboard. The side airbags knocked the grinder twins' heads together. Jack shoved the driver out of the way, pushed open the door, and dove.

His belly flop onto the pavement wouldn't have won any style points, but it did set him free.

6

Gentrification set its sights on Valencia Street long after Jack moved out of the Mission and now he did a double take every time he visited. A barrio turned gourmet ghetto, it had more restaurants crowding its blocks than any other neighborhood in the city. Even the old Mexican food joints had gone upscale by selling gluten-free tacos stuffed with kale and free-range chicken. Hark's grandma's restaurant was the exception. The décor at Abuelita's hadn't changed in twenty years and the food stayed traditional. Her frijoles were cooked in lard and the tripe in her Sunday menudo was always fresh. It was still the best hangover cure ever invented.

Hark used the restaurant's bar as his front office. He greeted Jack with a whistle and handed him a frosty bottle of Pacifico. "Must've been some anniversary party last night. Those scratches on your neck and love bite under your eye? That Katie's one passionate *chica*. All due respect."

Jack took a stool and motioned toward his face. "These are courtesy of Sinclair Huntington's hired hands. They took me out to Candlestick and tried to bury me there."

"Those dudes from the other day?" Hark pulled a sawed-off

shotgun from beneath the bar. "Time to saddle up, *ese*. Teach those motherfuckers a lesson about respect."

"Finding the chips will school Huntington and his boys plenty."

"They know you're looking for them?"

"If they didn't then, they might now. They're after Brad. Find out how much he talked."

"You any closer to ID'ing the ship they're coming in on?"

"Not yet, but there's a party tonight that could shed some light. Huntington will be there. Maybe if I can rattle him, he'll let something slip."

"What kind of party?"

"The exclusive kind. Wanna go?"

"What do I got to wear?"

Jack tipped his beer bottle at the shotty Hark was cradling. "That and a couple of bandoliers. You'll blend right in."

Hark grinned. "Now you're talking."

Jack filled him in on what he'd found out so far about cargo manifests from Wonder Boy and gave a playback on the dustup with Cutler and the oversized winch winders.

"Kinda strange Huntington playing it this way," Hark said. "Didn't take him for the sort to go rough and tumble from the get-go."

Jack nodded. "Does seem out of character. But Brad's become a loose end."

"You getting the best of them out at the 'Stick means you became one too. They don't know what you know."

"That can be an advantage."

"A dangerous one, *vato*."

"There's something else about this score that doesn't sit right. I can feel it." Jack sucked on a slice of fresh lime and then took a pull of his Pacifico.

"What, he grow bored making billions and now needs some

kind of joyride? That's some sick shit. Like those movie stars shoplifting a bra even though they get millions to take theirs off."

"Huntington's going to need a lot more chips than a container full to meet demand once he shows them off at the gamer convention," Jack said. "He either stole more than the Fangs are admitting to or he's got a way to duplicate them himself."

"The rich always find a way to get richer." Hark opened a bottle of beer. He flicked the cap and watched it spin like a top on the bar. "You ever miss the old days?"

"Sure, sometimes. Taking something off somebody who didn't deserve it was always a rush. But staying honest, well, that keeps me pretty busy. Doesn't leave much time for dwelling on what once was."

Hark nodded. "I hear you. But sometimes... I mean, it's not the stealing cars or busting heads over whose block is whose I'm talking about. It's the freedom I miss. The respect I got. Nowadays I cruise my neighborhood and the people moved in round here look at me like I'm some kinda clown in a clown car. They don't get it. Low lows been around forever. We go way back. To the pachucos and zoots. Riding low in a cherry car is all about pride."

Jack tipped his bottle at him. "Neighborhood's changed. My old man was still alive? He wouldn't recognize it."

"Mine neither. Not that I ever knew him. You know what they're charging for rent around here? Like New York. Even more. My building? Apartment next to me they're sleeping four to a room. And I'm not talking about illegals neither. They're all rich techies with college degrees. All they do is live and breathe computer stuff. Those companies down in Silicon Valley? They're running hundreds of buses between there and here every day. Got air conditioning and Wi-Fi and everything. The dudes all want to live here in the Mission so the companies bus 'em for free."

"Things change," Jack said. "Life goes on."

"My point exactly," Hark said. "Everybody's getting rich off high tech. Dudes that moved here. My *abuela* cooking for them in the restaurant here. Huntington and the Fangs and those chips. Everybody's getting something."

Jack grinned. "You sure took a long time getting to it. You want to know if I'm planning to do more than just find the chips and tell Jimmie and his dad where they're at."

"Just saying," Hark said. "Everybody's getting rich and it sure sounds like there's a lot of chips coming this way. Who's going know when we find them, a box or two don't fall out of the container before we tell the Fangs where they're at?"

"I can't do that." Jack crossed his arms.

"Because of your brother-in-law? You think the Fangs would take it out on him they find out the load came up short?"

"Because of Katie." Jack eyed Hark. "And what about you? You're a businessman now. You got a shop. Employees. Customers. You want to risk all that?"

Hark thought on it. He raised his beer to his lips and drained the bottle in a single gulp. "I got to tell you, *ese*, who knew going straight was going be such hard work."

7

When Jack and Hark arrived at Moscone Center for the game developer convention's opening night gala, the plaza out front of the main exhibit hall's front doors was jammed with people of all shapes and sizes and colors and sexual orientations.

"Looks like Halloween on steroids," Hark said as they got in line behind three Master Chiefs, a couple of Lara Crofts, a party of Links, and a guy in full Kratos regalia.

"I told you that you could've worn the bandoliers and nobody would've given you a second glance," Jack said.

Hark grinned. "I love this town."

They entered the hall, threaded the crowd, and reached the escalators that lead to an invitation-only private ballroom. There was plenty of security, but Jack and Hark wore laminated VIP passes. Getting them was easy. Jack didn't need to call Henri LeConte to forge them; real ones were for sale on Craigslist. At the top of the escalator they were greeted by a pair of rent-a-cops wielding handheld scanners.

"Looks like a wine and cheese crowd up here," Hark said with a frown. "I hope they got *cerveza*."

Millions of twinkling LEDs hung from the ceiling of the private ballroom. The ersatz starlight provided a backdrop for holographic images of other worlds flashing from multiple projectors and a playlist of soundtracks from megahit electronic games blared from speaker towers.

"Huntington's here somewhere," Jack said. "You go left and I'll take right. If you spot him, come find me."

Hark grinned. "Sure thing, *jefe*." He marched straight to the nearest bar.

Jack started on his side of the room. The food tables were organized by cuisine. An ice sculpture carved in the likeness of Jill Valentine from Resident Evil served as the centerpiece of a martini bar. A dozen guys sporting carefully groomed three-day beards crowded around it, ogling the statue's curves.

"Get real," Jack said.

He didn't get two steps before a woman blocked his path. Her long black hair was pinned up with ivory chopsticks and she was wearing a midnight-blue cheongsam with a plunging neckline. She clutched a martini. The edge of the glass was kissed with red lipstick.

"You don't fantasize about her like the rest of the man-boys?" she asked, her dark eyes reflecting the twinkle of the LEDs.

"A little on the frosty side for my taste."

She gave Jack an appraising look. "And what is that?"

"Flesh and blood with an on and off switch that doesn't require a plug."

"Ah. A humanist. How novel." She gave the martini another kiss.

Jack calculated the diamonds in her drop earrings, pendant necklace, and bracelet at twenty carats easy and guessed she was either the CEO of Blue Nile or someone close to her had a thing for bling and the checkbook to go with it.

"I'm guessing you don't spend a lot of time playing *Halo*," he said, snatching a martini off the bar.

"I prefer grown-up toys."

"This is the investor and owner crowd here. Which are you?"

"Both."

"Impressive. What kind of companies?"

"The bigger the better." She paused. "I find size matters."

Her earrings were in the shape of double-8s. So was the diamond pendant that kept falling into her cleavage, as was the pattern of her diamond bracelet. Lucky 8 8.

Jack nodded toward the jewels and said, "*Ba shi ba.*"

Her slashes of eyebrows arched. "You speak Mandarin?"

"I've learned a few phrases along the way, but mostly I know good fortune when I see it."

She caressed her pendant, the jeweled equivalent of a rabbit's foot. "Perhaps it's your lucky night."

"I'm lucky every night," he said.

"Meaning you're married."

"Correct."

"Happily?"

"Very. And you?"

Her smile turned pained. "Unluckily. Unhappily. And very."

As she said it Jack recognized her. "You're Mai Huntington, aren't you?"

Her eyes flashed. "Why? Are you a friend of Sinclair's?"

"Never been introduced. I heard your husband described as a genius but here he left you all by yourself. That's not very smart in my book."

She sipped her martini. "Sinclair is all about business all the time and this is business."

"His priorities are misaligned. Mind me asking how you two met?"

"I was running my own real estate consulting firm in Hong

Kong. He needed office space for his China operations. I broke Business 101's cardinal rule: never fall in love with a client."

"And now you've fallen out of it."

"My husband is brilliant but not when it comes to people. You run a business and own a building, not your spouse."

"Any hope of fixing it?"

She shook her head and then sipped her martini again. "I plan to return to Hong Kong and my life."

"And give up all you have here? The news articles say you're in charge of worldwide operations."

Mai's eyes flashed again. "I am capable of looking after myself. I always have. I was born in Guangdong, but my parents traded me for the chance for a son. When I was eight I escaped the orphanage and went to Hong Kong. I graduated from cleaning hotels to managing them. By the time I was twenty-three, I owned two storefronts in Lan Kwai Fong and an apartment building in Kowloon. I'll be fine."

"Sorry," Jack said quickly. "I didn't mean to suggest you were the type to hang around just because your husband controlled the checkbook."

"You mean as Sinclair's other wives did. One thing about living on the streets of Hong Kong and becoming successful in real estate? You learn how to negotiate a contract."

"Including a prenup." Jack gave a mock bow. "I'm impressed. I didn't think anybody got the better end of a business deal with Sinclair Huntington."

"Nothing slips by me," Mai said with a smile. She drained the rest of her martini and the plump olive passed neatly between her lips. She chewed, swallowed, and then opened her mouth. The olive was gone but the pimento lay unbitten on the tip of her tongue.

Before Jack could say anything more the crowd surged, pushing them close. Her eyes locked on his, but he was concentrating on the fingers that were locked viselike around his arm.

"Mr. McCoul, is it? I see you have met my wife."

Sinclair Huntington had Cutler in tow. The ugly sailor owned the fingers digging into Jack's flesh. A welt on Cutler's cheek didn't help his looks any. It was the diameter of a car's coffee cup holder.

"Call me, Jack," he said. "And tell Ruddy Face here the training wheels came off long ago. I can stand all by myself."

Huntington held his smile, but there were razorblades lurking behind it. He gave Cutler a nod and the thug's grip loosened.

"The Mrs. and I were getting acquainted," Jack said.

"Is that a fact?" Huntington placed a possessive palm against the middle of her back. "Mai is not only exquisite, but exceptional. Are you not, my dear?" His voice reminded Jack of an oil slick. "She is in charge of all of my day-to-day operations."

"Don't you mean *our* operations?" Jack winked at Mai. "Community property laws being what they are in California."

Huntington continued to hold the smile. "Are you an attorney, Mr. McCoul, as well as a..."

"Opportunist?" Jack returned the smile. "Do those operations include fabrication of a new generation of self-healing smart chips?"

Huntington had a good poker face but Jack could spot a tell on Mount Rushmore. "I never discuss business with a stranger," Huntington said, "but I do enjoy talking about sailing. Have you ever been to South Africa?"

"Can't say that I have."

Huntington removed his hand from his wife's back and tugged on the cuffs of a crisp, white long-sleeved shirt. It was fastened by gold cuff links featuring onyx double-8s. "My profession may be high technology but my passion is high-stakes cup racing. One of my favorite courses is off Cape Town where the Atlantic and Indian Oceans meet. The winds are unpredictable and the waters boast the largest concentration of great white sharks in the world. Beautiful creatures. Fearsome predators. But along with sharks come remoras—pathetic little parasites that stick to the sides of the sharks and feed off the scraps the great white hunters leave behind. Occasionally, a remora will attach itself to the hull of my racing yacht. I have a special boathook I use to dislodge them. The barbed point is razor sharp but when handled properly, the hook will not scratch the fiberglass."

The Sultan of Silicon Valley paused. "I cannot say the same is true for the poor remora." Then he palmed his wife's back again and steered her away.

Cutler stepped close to Jack. "We're not finished. I still need to find your little brother. I'm coming after you."

"In what? First you lose Brad and then you crash a SUV. Come on, Ruddy. The way you're going, Huntington won't trust you with a BART ticket."

Cutler cocked his fist but before he could swing, a big hand grabbed his shoulder and spun him around.

"Cool it, *pendejo*, or I'll *Call of Duty* your ass."

Hark gave Cutler a shove, sending him crashing into the martini bar. The bro-grammers with three-day beards shrieked as the glacial Jill Valentine wobbled off her pedestal and shattered into ice cubes.

"*Call of Duty*?" Jack asked as Cutler skulked off.

Hark shrugged. "Hey, sometimes I got to baby-sit my kid nephew. He makes me play it with him."

Moscone Center was a few blocks from home as the pigeon

flies, and Jack found an unlocked door near the bottom of the escalator and took a shortcut across the South Exhibit level. He was halfway across the cavernous hall when the sound of quickening footsteps echoed behind him.

"Police. Hold it right there."

The shout brought Jack to a halt. He'd learned long ago there were three *R*s when it came to cops with guns: no running, resisting, or ripping them off. Most important, never give them an excuse to make a mistake. It was hard to register a complaint with a bullet in your back.

"Sorry, must've taken a wrong turn," he said.

Two of SFPD's finest, drawing overtime providing security for the gamer convention, had their hands on the butts of their service weapons. One of the cops was speaking into his collar mic. "We got him, Inspector. Roger that. We'll hold him til you get here."

The other cop—big, blond, and blockheaded—sneered at Jack. "Man, you are fucked big time."

Jack raised a brow. "Sounds like someone missed sensitivity training class."

The blond cop rocked forward on the balls of his feet. "What's that supposed to mean?"

The cop with the mic intervened. "Search him, Carter."

"Grab the wall and spread 'em," the blond cop said.

It was about what Jack expected. Though he played spider and kept his feet wide apart, the blond cop kicked his insoles and patted him down. Abalone steaks got softer treatment.

"He's clean," Carter told his partner. He yanked Jack's wallet from his pocket and extracted the driver's license.

Jack heard a new set of footsteps behind him and then a familiar voice. "How you doing, Jack?"

Still facing the wall, Jack said, "What happen, Terry? They

bust you to herding drunken cats? Keep the conventioneers from getting pickpocketed while they're getting blown?"

"Smart mouth, dumb move, as always. You haven't changed since kindergarten," Inspector Terry Dolan said.

Terry and Jack had been butting heads since they could crawl. Their dads were brothers in arms—meaning they bent their elbows together at United Irish Cultural Center get-togethers. Jack and Terry would get warehoused in the meeting hall's basement with the rest of the fire fighters' and police officers' brats while their parents were upstairs pounding down boilermakers and singing along to the Chieftains.

Terry was an altar boy then and even more so when he and Jack attended St. Joseph's together. While Jack didn't follow in his father's footsteps, Terry couldn't wait to join his on the police force. Eamon Dolan, better known on the street as Demon Eamon, was an old-school beat cop—meaning he was a cop who beat. Once Terry graduated from the academy, he started climbing the ladder as fast as he could, moving from patrol to robbery homicide. He had his eye on the big *C*—captain—and then commander and then chief.

"Mind if let go of the wall?" Jack said. "I'm pretty sure it won't fall."

"Be my guest."

Jack turned around. A flash went off. Terry was holding up his phone. Jack blinked away the light and said, "If you wanted to tag me on Facebook, I could've sent you a picture of me sitting on a white sand beach drinking a cold beer, palm trees in the background."

"This will be the first in a series," Terry said. "Next one is of you in the backseat of a squad car. Then behind bars downtown. Then in an orange jumpsuit. In the bus heading to Quentin. Then with a cellmate named Cornfed who's looking for a new wife. I'm going to deliver them to Katie. Show her what a stand-up guy you are. Remind her of the biggest mistake she made in her life."

"You mean not dumping you sooner?"

As soon as he said it, Carter whipped his Maglite from the loop on his belt and cracked it across Jack's hip.

It was common knowledge on both sides of the blue line that Katie had left Terry for Jack. The reason she went to Kathmandu was to decide if she loved Terry enough to spend the rest of her life as a cop's wife. When Katie and Jack locked eyes in that tearoom, it was like one of those nature movies where the couple blindly paddles a canoe over a waterfall. They fell so hard it washed everyone who'd come before out of their minds. Katie forgot she'd been dating a cop until they got home and Terry came looking for her.

The night he knocked on her door, he found Jack sitting on the couch. Jack didn't have much time to marvel at the fates because Terry was pulling his gun. He might have pulled the trigger too if Jack hadn't thrown a perfect strike with a little stone Buddha statue. Later, Jack called it Zen and the art of ex-boyfriend maintenance.

The blow to Terry's forehead knocked him out cold. Jack pocketed the rounds before splashing water on his old schoolmate's face. When he returned Terry's weapon, Jack also gave him his word he wouldn't press charges as long as Terry stayed lost. Jack had held up his end of the bargain but Terry couldn't. He'd made it his life's ambition to take Jack down and win back Katie.

Terry said, "If you were a stand-up guy you'd let her go."

"That's your problem," Jack said. "You still think it's you and me that have a say in what Katie wants. That's why she didn't want to marry you in the first place. Too many handcuffs."

Terry turned red. "Take him to the hall and book him."

"For what?" Jack said. "I have a lawyer who bought a winery

in Napa from all the settlement money he's made off false arrests."

"Trespassing, fraud and larceny, for starters." Terry stuck out his chest. "A guest at the private party upstairs says you were trying to con him. You're looking at multiple felonies."

Jack laughed. "Try harder. I didn't even sneeze on the sushi platter."

"I'm talking about a prominent citizen. He's going to file a complaint."

"Anyone complaining should be me for the price I had to pay for the ticket. Those drinks had more water in them than San Francisco Bay."

Terry's face wrinkled with disgust. "You make me sick. You're nothing but a parasite."

Being called that twice in a night? Jack didn't buy it for a minute. "Who are you working for?" he said.

"The people of San Francisco." Terry stuck out his chest again.

"You mean Sinclair Huntington. He sent you after me, didn't he?"

"I don't know what you're talking about."

"Tell me, Terry, is it hard looking in the mirror and seeing that halo around your neck?"

The detective turned to the two cops. "I said cuff him."

Carter grabbed Jack's arm and twisted it behind his back, but the other cop's eyes were shining with doubt. "What are we taking him in for, Inspector? I mean, Carter and me, we're the ones have to go on the record as the arresting officers."

No cop wanted a false arrest in their jacket. At the beginning of every shift, the duty sergeant always warned them to treat paperwork like it was Charmin Ultra Soft. Use too much and clog the crapper and it would be them manning the plunger and scrub brush.

Terry hesitated. It only lasted a second but so did an atom splitting. He yanked the laminated VIP pass hanging from Jack's neck and brandished it in his face. "I'm going to run this and if I find it's a counterfeit, I'm going to bring you in myself. Count on it."

"I'll be sure to say hello to Katie for you," Jack said as the detective walked away.

8

It was half past noon when Jack walked to the Ferry Building at the foot of Market Street. The place was hopping with office workers who'd come to grab lunch in the restaurants and shop for fresh produce at the outdoor farmer's market. Jack worked his way through the crowd and found Katie standing beneath a white umbrella that shaded a stall selling kiwis. Bunches of radicchio and kale were stuffed in a canvas bag slung over her shoulder.

"How's my favorite fanny, farmer?" he asked, putting his hand on her rear.

Katie held up a slice of kiwi she took from a sampling plate. "Take a bite. It's sweet and succulent."

"You or the fruit?"

"Shush." She pushed the slice between his lips. "I thought I'd make winter soup with acorn squash and a fresh salad for dinner tonight."

Jack swallowed the kiwi. It was more tangy than sweet. "To go with a couple of steaks, right?"

Katie mock groaned. "I can hear your arteries clogging from here."

"Well, we need protein after our anniversary. How about some fresh oysters? We can grab a stool at Hog Island's bar. They have that Fumé Blanc you like."

"Ooh, that does sound delish. Here, pay for the kiwis and pick out some basil and blood oranges for the salad. I'll meet you inside." Katie handed him the canvas bag and disappeared into the main hall's entrance.

Jack forked over some bills to the kiwi grower and moved down the aisle in search of fresh herbs and citrus. A wiry man with slicked back hair stepped in front of him.

"Well, what do we have here? If it isn't backstabbing, double-crossing Jack McCoul. Care for a carrot, Jack? They snap when you bite." The man grabbed a carrot from a seller's table and chomped it. He chewed noisily, bits of orange sticking to his pointy teeth.

Jack looped the straps of the canvas bag around his wrist. "Hello, Brix. When did they let you out?"

Jack hadn't seen Caspar Brixton since he'd been sent to prison for a scam that was a bust from the start. Brix was running a long con that was short on strategy as well as finesse. Jack made one of the biggest mistakes in his career: he agreed to help a grifter he barely knew. Before Jack could straighten out Brix's con, the mark got wise and tipped off the law. An undercover cop was inserted into the play. When Brix told Jack about the mark's new business partner, Jack took a walk and told him to do the same. Brix wouldn't listen and wound up doing a five-year stretch.

"These are Nantes carrots," Brix said. "I know because I know my produce. Got to know it personal at Soledad working in the prison's fields. Summer time? They had us picking even when it got to 110 degrees. Therapeutic vocational training is what they called it. As if the best thing you can hope for when you get out of the joint is a job as a wetback. Ever smell that stink broccoli gets if you leave it on the burner too long? That's what it's like in the fields." He waved the Nantes. "I love carrots but broccoli? I like to gag."

Jack eyed Brix carefully. The stint in prison didn't mellow him any. His eyes were more beady, his pointed teeth more yellow, his once soft body was lean and drawn as sinew. Aryan Brotherhood tattoos covered his forearms. A swastika, a skull, SS lightning bolts.

Jack pushed past him. "You should try Italian broccoli with balsamic and garlic. Might change your mind."

Brix grabbed another carrot, this one thick and purple, and held it like a shiv. "You owe me, McCoul. You owe me five years of my life. You owe me the two hundred grand I was going to take off that mark. You owe me a new opportunity to make it right."

Jack tested the heft of the canvas bag, ready to swing it if it came to that. He wished Katie had bought grapefruit or apples. "I warned you the mark made your play. Whenever a new character you didn't write in yourself enters the stage, it's a sure sign you've got the law in the audience. You always drop and walk, no matter how big the prize."

Brix started tossing the purple carrot from hand to hand. "Five years inside, a man has a lot of time to think. In his cell, at chow, spearing new fish in the shower. Especially when hoeing peas in the hot sun. You may have walked, McCoul, but not before you talked. The case they had on me? Their information was so good they could describe the dreams I had the night before. How did they know all that unless someone told them?"

"Sounds to me you talk in your sleep."

A woman with dark hair and a peasant blouse was sitting on a stool behind the table full of produce. "Mister, are you going to buy my carrots? We're certified organic and our farm is very small. We can't afford too many free samples."

Brix brandished the carrot. "Shut up or I'll shove this up your hole."

Jack stepped between them. "You don't want to cause a scene, Brix. You break parole, they'll send you back. Only this time it'll be to San Quentin, where the only garden is the potted plant on the warden's desk."

Brix jammed his hand in his pocket and pulled out a handful of coins. He chucked them at a basket. Then he raised his chin. The chords in his neck stretched as tight as the strings on a harp. His beady eyes flickered. "You owe me an opportunity, McCoul. If you're working a play right now, you got to let me in. Otherwise, go find me one. You got to make things right." He jammed the purple tuber against Jack's heart. "I'll be in touch."

JACK JOINED Katie at the restaurant's oyster bar. She started in about Brad.

"I texted and called him but he never got back to me. You said he was fine when you left him in Chinatown. I'm worried about him." She took a sip of the crisp white wine and shivered.

"He's probably tied up doing something. If it will make you feel any better, I'll swing by and check on him after lunch. Okay?"

"Would you? I'm teaching a class this afternoon and won't have time."

Jack sprinkled an oyster with horseradish and slurped it from the half shell. "Which one?"

"It's my women's kundalini yoga workout."

"That's the class where you have them alternate between deep breathing, fantasizing, and Kegel exercises, right?"

Katie turned defensive. "It's not a joke. The class is very

popular. Women need to be in control of every part of their body."

Jack raised his wine glass. "Don't forget, practice makes perfect."

~

AFTER LUNCH, Katie went home while Jack took a walk. Chinatown and Brad could wait. He needed more information about ships coming into San Francisco Bay. His phone rang when he was halfway down the Embarcadero. Caller ID was blocked but he picked up anyway.

"Speak," he said.

"Mr. McCoul?"

"Why, Mrs. Huntington. What a surprise."

"You recognize my voice?"

"You make quite an impression."

She paused. "I'm told you're a con man."

"I've been called a lot of things."

"Is it true?"

"You should ask the guy who sits on a mountaintop twiddling his navel. He says truth is relative."

"You're being difficult, Mr. McCoul."

"First off, it's Jack. Second, you called me. Is there something I can help you with?"

Despite the squawk of seagulls and chatter of people strolling along the waterfront, Jack could hear her take a deep breath.

"You said something to my husband last night which was quite disconcerting."

"What can I say? I flunked cotillion. If I offended you, I apologize. If I offended him, well, that's another matter altogether."

"It was about a new line of self-healing microchips."

"What about them?"

"I knew nothing about them."

"Why tell me? Ask your husband about them."

"You're not listening. I've heard nothing about them and I should have. I'm chief operating officer. I checked our books. I talked to our people in research and development, in manufacturing, and in mergers and acquisitions. Nobody knows anything about them. If anybody should, I should."

Jack stopped walking. He sat on the edge of a granite planter and faced the bay.

"Are you telling me this as head of operations or as a wife?" he asked.

Mai Huntington took another deep breath. "Both. Well, primarily as wife."

"Why? Are you worried he might be doing something illegal and get you thrown in jail with him?"

She laughed. "Men like Sinclair don't go to jail. They have other people put in jail."

"You're planning to divorce him, aren't you? What we were talking about at the gala. Community property, negotiating. You got yourself an ironclad prenup and now you think he's building a business on the side and keeping it off the marital books."

There was no reply. Jack held the phone away from his ear and checked the screen to make sure they hadn't been disconnected.

Finally she spoke. "You're smarter than you act. I sensed as much."

"Wait a minute, Mai. You don't mind if I call you Mai, right? You got the wrong impression. If you're looking for a divorce lawyer, I can recommend one. If you're looking for a private eye to catch your husband doing the business equivalent of screwing his mistress, well, before I retired I worked the opposite side of the law enforcement street, if you catch my meaning. I could get a name or two for you, though."

"I don't want to talk to anybody else. I need someone just like you."

"No, you don't. I can give you a million reasons why you don't."

"And I will give you a million reasons why you should. Each with a dollar attached to it. Do you realize what is at stake in a divorce settlement with someone of Sinclair's means?"

"If it's anything like your husband's previous trips down the aisle, I got a pretty good idea."

"Those women settled for pennies. I'm not about to make the same mistake."

"I hope that includes not doing what the first Mrs. Huntington did."

"You don't know my husband. That poor woman may have shot herself but, believe me, Sinclair spent years loading the gun."

"Not exactly a great sales line to convince me to help you."

"From what I've learned, you're not the kind of man who is afraid of someone like my husband."

"What is it exactly you're asking?"

"I'll pay you to help me prove Sinclair is hiding a hugely profitable new venture. I'm entitled to half. That which you discover will give me all the leverage I require."

"And how do you suggest I do that?"

"Please, Mr. McCoul. Jack. It's not like I haven't done my research. I know of what you are capable. Come to my home tonight and we will discuss it. I'll make our agreement formal and secure your services with a retainer. A very generous one."

"And your husband?"

"What of him?"

"I doubt he'll roll out the welcome wagon when I knock on the door."

"Don't worry about Sinclair. He's on an overnight cruise with his fellow Franciscan Yacht Club members. They sail up the delta with a full crew of attractive and willing young women."

"Will Cutler be manning the sails?"

"I presume so."

"What about personal security and staff at the house?"

"They have the night off."

"That's convenient," Jack said.

Mai gave him the address. "I will expect you at ten," she said, her voice crisp.

Before he could say no, the phone went dead. It was as good a negotiating tactic as any.

9

San Francisco's piers poked into the bay like fingers grabbing at passing ships. One of the shortest was Pier 22½. It was built that way on purpose to give the two fireboats docked alongside faster access to open water.

"As I live and breathe," Marquis Williams said with a wide grin as he waved Jack into Station 35's open truck bay. The red and white pumper parked inside was receiving a wax job from two guys who were June and July in the annual fundraiser calendar for the fire department.

"I was passing by and thought I'd see if they finally pensioned you off," Jack said.

He braced for the hard squeeze that came from a man who was pushing the wrong side of fifty but could still handle a three-inch hose and split open a solid door with a swing of a pick head axe.

The fireboat captain laughed. "Let them try, but I'm head of the local now. They know which side their sourdough's buttered on. How about you? How's tricks?"

"Still juggling them," Jack said with a shrug.

Marquis Williams was wise to some of Jack's history, not all, but he'd heard enough to know Jack wasn't a nine-to-fiver. "And Katie? As bright and beautiful as ever, I'm sure. She going to make me a godfather soon?"

"The sun and moon check with her before rising and setting, don't they? And as for the other part, well, we're still in spring training, don't you know?"

Marquis laughed behind a moustache that was more ash than soot. "You sound like your old man laying on that old country brogue shit. The younger brothers use to take offense when Gavin did that, but I always told them you put out a fire and when the smoke clears, look around at everyone's face before they get a chance to wash off. Who gets the last laugh then?"

Jack had heard him give the line plenty of times before. Still, he grinned.

"Yeah, your old man was a solid fireman," Marquis said. "Solid father too. Seems like yesterday Gavin would have the pack of you kids here for his annual family fishing trip."

Marquis was being generous. The truth was Jack's father was a first-class son of a bitch and a two-fisted boozer who spent more time at the firehouse than he did at his family's house. He favored five-alarms, banquets at the United Irish Cultural Center and Giants home games, not necessarily in that order. He hated dalmatians. The way he saw it, kids were a Catholic requirement but a damn nuisance all the same, especially after Jack's mother died of cancer. It was then Jack and his brothers and sister learned how much their mother shielded them from their father's true nature. PTA meetings were for suckers. If you couldn't cook your own meals, you had no business eating. You wanted new shoes, get yourself a job.

To Gavin, Christmas was an opportunity for collecting easy overtime. The only family occasions he celebrated were the kids' birthdays—all together and all on the same day. He'd take them for a cruise on one of Station 35's fireboats and while the kids trolled for stripers, Gavin would crush beer cans and tell them how unlucky they were. There was never a cake and the only thing they ever caught was a bad case of sunburn.

"Speaking of fishing trips, any chance for a trip down memory lane?" Jack asked Marquis.

The fireboat captain grinned. "You don't have to ask. Follow me."

They walked onto the pier. It smelled of creosote and seagull shit. The *Phoenix* and *Guardian* were tied to the dock, a row of enormous truck tires serving as fenders. The *Phoenix* was Jack's favorite. Built in '54, it was still a workhorse, a battleship really. Its battery of monitors could blast nine thousand gallons a minute and the ship was able to pump seawater on flames for twenty-four hours straight without having to refuel.

Jack and Marquis scrambled over the gunwales and climbed onto the bridge. Marquis motioned for Jack to sit at the chart table while he took his customary seat behind the wheel. He patted the oak spokes lovingly. "I've seen it all from here. Every wharf fire, every burning yacht, all the poor bastards who took the long step off the Golden Gate and wound up floating face down. Always face down, even the women."

Marquis stared at the bay. "The night of the '89 quake, we kept the marina from burning to a cinder. No bragging. Just fact. Trained our monitors on the big houses across Marina Green and kept pouring it on. When we started running low on fuel to power the pumps, we scrambled aboard all those fancy boats tied at the Franciscan's private dock and helped ourselves to their tanks using an Oklahoma credit card."

Jack gazed out the windshield, seeing it as Marquis described it, picturing Sinclair Huntington and his fleet of multimillion-dollar yachts moored there. "You guys rule the bay." Jack snapped a salute.

Marquis chuckled. "It's a fact. We're fire fighters first and the department signs our pay slips, but we answer to the Port of San Francisco. We hold the permit on every fire extinguisher on every tub on the bay and along with inspecting those, we got to check every piling, every wharf and every tar-papered shack built on top. Ever since the City of Oakland ran into budget problems and had to dry dock the *Sea Wolf*, we've had to cover it all. San Francisco, Sausalito, Richmond, Berkeley, Oakland—you name it."

Jack whistled. "You got to be careful you don't drown in an ocean of paperwork. They give you a list of each ship coming into the bay?"

"They come and go nonstop. Like blood in a vein."

"And what they're carrying, huh? So you know ahead of time if it's oil or chemicals or such. You don't want any surprises if you have to pour water on it"

Marquis nodded. "It's all computerized, so we don't have to check manifests unless we need to. A ship hits a pylon or engine starts smoking and we get dispatched. By the time we get to the scene, they already got the list blinking right here."

The fireboat captain pointed to the computer screen that was built into the chart table Jack was standing next to. "You wouldn't believe everything that gets shipped here these days. Even toilet paper. Comes all the way from mills in Papua, New Guinea. Seems like the only thing made in the US anymore is fire. Good work to be in. Plenty of job security." He took a breath and gave Jack an expectant look. "So, you ever think of taking up the ax and hat like your dad, may he rest in peace?"

As he said it the battle-hardened skipper bowed his head. It was clean shaven and the wheelhouse's overhead lights reflected on it like stars in the night. Marquis was picturing the formal portrait that hung on the battalion headquarters's wall of fallen heroes. The official story was Gavin was searching for unaccounteds in a four-alarmer that was racing through a Noe Valley apartment building. The floor collapsed and the whole thing went up around him. Jack never bought it. He always figured his dad was doing what he'd been doing for years—using the smoke as a screen so he could through dresser drawers and pocket loose cash and jewelry.

Jack had come across the stash one day. When he asked his father about it, Gavin's answer was a right to the jaw and a left to the solar plexus. "Mind your own fookin' business," he said. "You don't know what it takes to raise a motherless brood, put food on the table, save for your sister's wedding at Saint Joe's." Jack knew enough not to talk back. He never mentioned it again, not even to Katie. He also knew there wasn't much he could do about the genes he'd inherited, so Jack made a pledge to best his old man at his own game.

"You know how it is when your father plows a deep course," Jack said to Marquis. "You got to make your own path if you want to be your own man."

Marquis nodded. "Point taken. But you ever need help, any help at all, you know where to find us."

"Now don't I?" Jack said, plying on the brogue again. He clapped him on the shoulder and gave the *Phoenix's* chart table a pat for good luck too.

10

The #38 rumbled up Geary Boulevard, another one of San Francisco's grand thoroughfares named for an Irish pioneer. The deeper into the Richmond District the muni bus traveled, the grayer the sky turned. Jack got off at Twenty-fifth and walked to his sister's second-floor flat. He rang the bell and then tried the door. It was unlocked. The place was sunless and cramped and the green shag carpet smelled of cat piss and kids. Jack found Meaghan in the kitchen hunched over a greasy yellow Formica table. She was clutching a glass half-full of vodka mixed with sweetened powdered tea.

"Katie left a note on the fridge saying you called. Did he hit you again? Where is he?" Jack asked.

"The shit's late," Meaghan said as she focused on the glass. "Two weeks this time. I don't know how I'm going to feed the kids. Rent's already a month past. They're going to shut off the electricity any day now."

Jack could see her husband. Derrick usually wore a commemorative 49er jersey that showed off the twin tats on his forearms: old-fashioned oil wells spouting a gusher straddled by naked women with enormous breasts.

"So, where's Derrick?" he asked.

"How should I know? He only comes home to rifle through the cupboards and look for the grocery money. He even took the baby's silver baptism spoon and pawned it. He's a shit. I should've listened to you and never married him. Jesus, Jackie. What am I going to do?"

He cupped his sister's chin and lifted her head so he could look for bruises. It wouldn't be the first time he found them. "File for divorce, like I always tell you. You and the kids will be better off."

Meaghan shook her head. Her hair was dirty. When it was washed, it shined with three shades of red. Their father used to say it had more color than the flames he fought. She'd been a cheerleader once but that was a lifetime ago.

"I can't do that. The church forbids it," she said.

"But they're okay with him smacking you around, right?"

"Don't blaspheme."

"You need to make it legal to force him to pay child support."

"Derrick does what he can. I mean, sometimes. This is hard on him too. He has issues. He's trying to deal with them."

Jack blew out air. "M., listen to you. You're making excuses for him again. One breath you're calling Derrick a worthless sack of shit, the next you're nominating him for father of the year. How do you expect me to help you?"

Meaghan took a swallow and then fumbled for the pack of cigarettes next to the glass. She lit one and blew out smoke. "Don't make me ask, Jackie. Come on. A girl needs her pride."

Cereal bowls were piled in the sink. A cat was lapping sour milk out of one. Another cat was pawing at a greasy brown paper bag on the floor.

"What happened to the housecleaner?" Jack asked. "I send the service a check every month. They're supposed to come once a week. Give the place an industrial scouring. Remember? So you can spend the time looking for a job. So the kids don't get scabies or botulism."

"The maid's a lazy shit. She doesn't even scrub the sink or vacuum the floor."

"That's because she can't find them. Come on, M. I'm okay helping out but you got to help yourself."

Meaghan sucked on the cigarette and exhaled smoke through her nose. "You think it's easy raising three kids by yourself? Tell me, when do I have time to look for work?"

Jack plucked the glass off the table and tossed the contents over the dirty dishes. The splash scared away the cat.

"You need to clean yourself up. Scrub the house. Scrub yourself. Call that lawyer. File papers on Derrick and make it official. I'll pay the rent, make you square on all your bills. I'll give you a little something every month for the kids. Make sure they eat right, go to the doctor. In exchange, you find a job and take it. Then think about finding a good man who will love you and take care of you, treat you and the kids with respect. Not smack you around."

Jack took a breath. On her deathbed his mother had asked him to look out for Meaghan. He tried his best, defending her honor though she deserved her reputation as Lay Again Meaghan. When their dad cashed it on the job, Jack stepped up and took over helping out with the bills. He was always the one there for her since she couldn't count on her other brothers. Patrick and Declan were dead to him. They'd sold the family house following their father's death and hocked all of its furnishings, right down to the family photos. Jack started college funds for Meaghan's kids the day they were born. He contributed to them regularly and never told his sister or Derrick about it, knowing if he did they'd plunder their children's savings.

Meaghan stood, wobbled over, and threw her arms around

his waist. "You're my favorite brother. You always have been. I love you. The kids adore you. Little Derrick asks every day when his Uncle Jackie is going to take him to another Giants game. The older he gets, the more he looks like you and Dad. You put a picture of you all together, it'd be like triplets."

"A regular rogue's gallery that would be." Jack patted his sister on the back. "I got to go." He pulled out his roll and peeled off three hundred-dollar bills. "I'll send your landlord, PG&E, and the phone company a check. Now tell me where Derrick is?"

Meaghan held her cigarette in the V between her fingers and sucked on it nervously. "I don't know. I'm not sure."

"Which is it? Don't know or not sure?"

"Going to see him won't do any good. He'll tell you to fuck off."

"So he tells me. He got a girl?"

She shook her head. "No, I don't think so. I'm not sure."

"Come on, M. Where he's hanging? I want to talk to him. Let him know I came by and saw you. That I'm going to help out any way I can. Help him too. Help him find a job."

"You'd do that for him?"

"He's the father of my nieces and nephew. He's my sister's husband." Jack couldn't bring himself to say brother-in-law.

Meaghan stubbed out the smoke. She looked nervously at the three hundreds and then the cabinet next to the sink where she kept the booze. "Try any of the pubs in the Avenues. The Plough, the Blackthorn, the 32."

Jack fanned the bills on the yellow Formica table. "Tell the kids hello for me." He started for the door. "And Meaghan?"

"Yeah, Jackie?"

"Wash your hair."

11

San Francisco had as many Irish pubs as it did Irish cops and fire fighters. Jack spent the rest of the evening searching for Derrick but if any of the bartenders knew where he was, they weren't saying.

It was closing in on 10 p.m., so Jack grabbed a taxi and had the driver let him off on the corner of Broadway and Divisadero. As soon as the cabbie pulled away, he walked up Broadway toward Broderick and the richest block in the city. Mansions lined both sides of the street. The houses were big with high walls and strong gates, the landscaping lush and well tended. The most opulent mansion was a three-story baroque French château with columns out front, high-arched windows, and a mansard roof. Jack didn't need to confirm the address to know he was at the right place. Sinclair Huntington's personal monument to himself was about as subtle as the Hollywood sign.

A circular drive paved with granite cobbles led to a front door the size of a cathedral's. Jack pushed a brass button and a chime sounded. He looked up. A wall-mounted security camera stared back. He gave it a smile and waited. A few minutes later he hit the brass button again. No one came. He waited a few more minutes, smiled at the camera again, and then pounded on the door. It was unlatched and swung inward.

"Hello? It's Jack McCoul. Anybody home?"

There was no Mai, no butler, no maid, no nobody. Not even a yappy little dog. Jack walked in.

The entry hall was the size of hotel lobby. The walls were polished marble. So was the floor. An island chain of oriental rugs led him past a series of empty rooms. He thought for sure he'd find someone in the kitchen—Huntington wouldn't pull a cork out of a bottle of wine himself—but no one was there.

A curved double stairway led upstairs. Jack took the right side and started climbing. Paintings hung on the wall, all originals and museum quality. Closed doors lined a long, wide hallway. It was *Let's Make a Deal* time. No one was behind doors one, two, three and four, but when he turned the handle to door number five, the smell of perfume and urine filled his nostrils.

Mai was lying on her stomach on a king-size bed. She wore an ebony sheath dress and black stiletto heels. Her head was twisted to the side, her eyes open. Her arms and legs were like those of a marionette with its strings cut.

Jack had seen bodies before. The first was his mother's. Her skin had been as thin and translucent as wax paper when cancer finally took her. Mai's was the opposite. It still showed color. He glanced around the room and wished he had a gun.

Her broken neck was surely not the result of suicide. No rope hung from the ceiling. No twisted bed sheet was tied to the headboard. Jack nodded to himself. Someone had strong-armed her from behind and twisted her head, snapping one of the delicate cervical vertebrates.

Years ago, when Jack was watching his mother die in her own bed, unhooked from machines as she had wished, he found a switch within himself that he could turn off to control his emotions. He flipped the switch now to keep from going to Mai and closing her eyes.

He made mental notes as he studied the death scene and then slowly backed out. Jack pulled the door closed and wiped the knob clean. He retreated down the hall, wiping all of the doorknobs. He wiped the banister too.

By the front door was a small room filled with electronic equipment. A computer monitor displaying eight split frames showed the front entrance, backyard, various rooms, and Mai lying dead on her bed. Jack's instincts were telling him to smash the system and get out as quickly as he could, but he ignored them. A few strokes of the keyboard and he was in control of the playback. He hit reverse and the monitor replayed his movements. And then the recording went blank. Whoever killed her had done what he did next. He hit delete and his presence, like that of the murderer's, was erased. He turned off the security system so it wouldn't record him leaving, wiped the keyboard, and left.

HARK FOUND him in a bar on Union Street a few blocks from the Huntington mansion. Jack was sitting at a table with a boilermaker in front of him.

"Got here as quick as I could, *ese*. What's the 911?"

The place was crowded with eager singles. Jack signaled the waitress for two more drinks. As soon as she delivered them and was out of earshot, he said, "Finding the chips play went capital."

Hark dropped the shot into the pint glass and watched the whisky stain the beer. He took a gulp and wiped his lips with the back of his hand.

"Who's dead?"

"Mai Huntington."

Hark nodded as if Jack had told him tomorrow would be chilly with winds out of the northwest. "I'm going ask it once because I got to, all due respect."

Jack didn't wait for the question. "It wasn't me. All I did was find her. Someone broke her neck. They may not have meant it to go that far but it did."

"This being where?"

"In her bedroom."

"You being there. In her bedroom."

"She'd called me earlier and set up a meet."

"And Katie?"

"What about her?"

"Hey, *vato*, I saw Huntington's wife at that gala for geeks, remember? She's mighty fine. Was." He gulped more of the boilermaker. "I'm not judging, you understand, why you happened to be in her bedroom."

"Turns out she was going to divorce Huntington and had a prenup. When I mentioned the chips at the gala, she put two and two together and figured out hubby was setting up a side business. She wanted me to prove it."

"She didn't know you were already looking for the chips?"

"If she did she didn't say so."

"You think she knew about Huntington taking them off the Fangs?"

"Who knows?"

"Sounds like Huntington found out she found out about his game to cut her out, and he whacked her. Husbands whack their wives all the time. Sometimes the other way 'round. Cops could see it that way."

"If Huntington killed her, then he did it by proxy. He's spending the night on a sailboat version of Bohemian Grove. He'll be alibied six ways to Sunday. Mai said it herself. Men like Huntington don't go to jail. They put other people in jail."

Hark skated his pint glass around. "When I was in the 'Stan I wasn't always sure what we were fighting for but I'll tell you one thing, I wished we done more to straighten out the way the men there treated women and little girls. Dude could kill a wife, a sister, a daughter just 'cause he thought she was looking at some other dude the wrong way. They didn't throw his ass in jail; they gave him a fucking medal. They called it honor killing."

"Different culture, different religion."

"Yeah, but that don't make it right no matter what god you pray to, what language you speak. And I don't care how bucks-up this Huntington dude is. He killed his wife, then he deserves a different kind of medal. The full-jacket kind."

"Proving he did it won't be easy," Jack said.

"But the cops are going to have to pin it on somebody," Hark said quietly. "That's what cops do."

Jack nodded. "You mean me." He toyed with his drink.

"You were the last person out the door." Hark studied Jack. "Anybody see you coming or going?"

"I took a cab there but got out a few blocks away. Still, the cops will canvas the cabbies and the driver will make me. That's why I chose this bar. It's nearby the house and me being here makes it reasonable doubt."

"But people got to remember you were here." Hark downed his boilermaker. "You already got a plan to make them remember, don't you?"

"It's a yuppie joint. We raise our voices loud enough, they'll piss their designer jeans."

Hark grinned. "So who gets to throw the first punch?"

Jack grabbed his drink and tossed it in Hark's face. "That's my wife you're talking about," he shouted, jumping up and knocking over his chair.

12

It was still early and the fog was pregnant with saltwater as Jack pounded along the Embarcadero. He wore an orange Giants cap pulled low, a pair of running shoes with neon green laces, and a San Francisco State sweatshirt that was already darkened with a saddle of sweat. Jack preferred exercising outdoors rather than on a conveyor belt. He started running while playing shortstop at St. Joseph's. The priests, who doubled as coaches, were always ordering the team to do laps around the bases—part training, part punishment, and partly because it meant supervising mandatory showers.

The fresh air helped clear Jack's head, which allowed him to focus on Mai's murder. If not Huntington, then who? A lover? A burglar? A disgruntled employee? A vendor who'd lost a contract? It was only a matter of time until the police hauled Jack in for questioning, and he needed facts before they did. Just as in running a con, it always paid to have more information than anyone else. It was the only way to stay in control of the action.

Jack reached Fisherman's Wharf with no more answers than when he had started, so he turned around and quickened his pace. When he reached his building, his sides were splitting and his breath came in deep gasps. He hesitated rather than going straight to the loft. Katie would be awake by now and he wasn't ready to face her yet. His muscles burned from the workout as much as his head ached from trying to decide what he was going to do next about the chips and Mai's murder. The steam room in the gym beckoned.

Though all the members of the gym lived no more than an elevator ride away, they all kept lockers. Jack didn't know what went on in the women's locker room—when he asked Katie, she gave him a sly look and said, "Wouldn't you like to see"—but the men's was a computer geek's fantasy. Hi-def flat screens were on every wall, along with PS's, a Wii, a row of work cubicles equipped with laptop hookups though no one ever let go of their smartphone, and even a couple of old-fashioned pinball machines. Jack swapped his sweats and shoes for a towel and took a seat on the top tier of the white-tiled steam room. He had the place to himself and he closed his eyes. The thick, moist air started to work its magic, loosening his muscles. He drifted, riding on a current of warm air that made him picture the humid and tropical-like Kathmandu Valley and a lush garden and temple that stood on the banks of the Bagmati River. It was where he first told Katie he loved her.

Jack felt the heat, smelled the lotus blossoms. The squeak of shower sandals followed by an equally squeaky voice pulled him back.

"Mr. McCoul, uh, Jack. Mind if I join you?"

Jack opened one eye and one-eightied the room. A slender figure dressed in a short terry cloth robe and blue rubber flip-flops wavered in the thick steam. It was Leonard Something-or-other. Skinny and pasty as a barista, Leonard was an obsessive compulsive gym rat. Every day he spent thirty minutes on the aerobic machines, followed by a ten-minute steam, ten-minute shower, and ten minutes checking e-mails as he pulled on his trademark Zuckerman hoodie.

"Climb on up, Leo," Jack said.

The first time he had met Leonard, Jack's old habits kicked into gear. Sensing an easy mark, he baited the hook by allowing Leonard to overhear him talking on his phone about an investment that couldn't miss. Leonard bit and the play nearly became another one of Jack's little slip-ups before he decided not to go through with it. Part of his decision had to do with the commitment he made to Katie, and part of it had to do with his own code. Leonard didn't fit the bill of a digital despot whose power and wealth came from breaking the rules. Now Jack needed to toss him back in the water without raising suspicion.

"I haven't seen you for a while," Leonard said as he inched forward, his hands out. His glasses were fogged up like a car windshield in a rock concert parking lot. "Have you changed your exercise regime or is business keeping you too busy?"

Jack sighed and rubbed his temples as he switched into his venture capitalist guise. "No time as of late. Wall-to-wall meetings. Chain smoking my cell all day. I start with the distributors in Taipei and follow the sun across the time zones. The manufacturers in Shenzhen. Call centers in Bangalore. Software designers in Prague. And then there are the Wall Street boys." He sighed again, this time more heavily. "It always comes to them, doesn't it?"

Leonard pumped his fist. "I hear you. Tech is, well, it's like life. It's 24-7."

Jack nodded as if Leonard spit out the fattest pearl ever. "True that, but would we have it any other way? Would we settle for anything less than creation? What fulfillment is there in standing still when you can be standing tall?"

Leonard gulped the 114 degree liquid air and coughed. He wiped his nose on the sleeve of his short robe. "I've been doing a lot of research. You're right. No one's heard anything about the start-up you were talking about. It's a total blue screen. The returns could be huge. I've made my decision. I want to invest."

Jack closed his eyes again and rolled his neck. It was as if he had all the time in the world, but really he was speed-reading the script for the play. Then he remembered. The scam was based on a nonexistent start-up with a pie-in-the-sky app Jack dreamed up. He opened his eyes slowly. "I'm sorry, Leo. On my 6 a.m. today, the underwriter boys at Morgan Stanley told me the Series A funding is fully subscribed." Jack paused for a few moments. Visions of his account in the Caymans growing fatter appeared in the steam. Try as he might, he couldn't help himself. "Or close to it."

Leonard sputtered. "What?"

The old familiar feeling came rushing back. "I'm sure I told you interest popped when people found out"—he made a show of looking around for anyone who might be lurking—"you-know-who came in as the lead angel investor. I can't mention his name out loud, you understand why, but Big Angel put in such a huge number the enterprise skipped seed and is going straight to Series A. There are already whispers it will go public faster than anything NASDAQ's ever seen. Fourth quarter, for sure. The underwriters are losing sleep trying to calculate valuation. Nobody wants another Facebook IPO on their sheet."

"You said they're close to locking down the Series A. That means there's still time," Leonard insisted as his puny body shook. "I don't need a seat on the board for it. I want in. No, I need in. You can do that for me, can't you?"

Katie's image flashed but Jack rationalized it wasn't a con unless he went through with it, and there was still plenty of time to pull the plug. He was just staying in shape, like a work out. Surely, she'd understand the difference.

"I suppose I can make a call," Jack said. "But I have to level with you, Leo. Big Angel is being hard-nosed about the number of additional investors. He didn't learn to share in kindergarten. He's insisting on minimums for entry and Omaha-style reporting—just a handshake and your word. It's all wire-transfer funds out and e-mail confirmation of shares in. Big Angel doesn't want anything to slow production, and that includes having to devote resources to paperwork."

Leonard's bottom lip quivered. "Meeting a minimum won't be a problem. My options vest in eight days. I'm on a scheduled sell plan. I have to put the proceeds somewhere."

The longer he spoke, the further Mai's murder and the chips sailed from view. The distraction was a relief. "Money sitting is money wasting," Jack said. "How could the next app be invented? Where would the next big thing come from if not for people like Mark, Sergei, Elon, and you? But eight days will be too late. If the door's still open, it's just a crack and it's closing fast."

Jack closed his eyes and rubbed his temples again. "Tell you what. I'll make the call and if there's still an opening, I can always put up my assets for you. You can sign your options over as collateral. As you said, it's only a few days until you get them anyway, right?"

"You'd do that for me?"

"I didn't get where I am by not following my gut. I have a good feeling about you, Leo. What goes around comes around. One day you'll be handing me the opportunity."

Leonard made a fist to bump knuckles. "All right."

Jack slid off the top-tier. He couldn't remember what Leonard had done to obtain so much money and so many stock options at such a tender age. "Remind me again, what space are you in?" he asked as he reached for the heavy glass door.

"Logistics and supply chain," Leonard answered. "I developed a new algorithm for QR codes when I was at Stanford.

Quick response bar codes? Only mine aren't two-dimensional, they're 3-D and have a terabyte of memory so you can input contents, origin, destination, customs forms, duty payments, and so on. Then I patented the methodology for implanting them with microtransponders. They'll take the place of the traditional serial shipping container code and the systems that track them."

"Shipping? You mean like UPS, FedEx?"

"Actually, our A-listers are the big international cargo fleets." Leonard's voice started picking up speed. "My 3-D QR transponders give the customer total control. They're self-scanning and trackable by GPS satellite no matter where they are on the planet. The data can be downlinked and uplinked to a mobile device in real time. A shipper can redirect a container with a click. The information is automatically re-registered in the new destination's port manifest database."

"Total control? You don't say."

Jack pulled open the door and the steam parted like a San Francisco fogbank being pushed aside by the bow of an inbound freighter.

13

The crowd at Pier Inn was usually too noisy to hear the wall-mounted TV, except when it was tuned to a Giants broadcast. But the season was still weeks away and all the local stations were covering the police press conference. Jack didn't pretend to be disinterested in the newscast. It would've made him stand out if he had. All eyes were on the screen. San Francisco was no stranger to murder, but this one had the makings of a crime that would wind up on the *Today* show. A sexy woman. A famous billionaire. A mansion in a neighborhood considered a world apart from the rest of the city.

Chief Liu wore dress blues and a stern look as he stood before the microphones. Word was he was already campaigning for mayor. His job was to reassure the public crime would not be tolerated. To underscore that fact, he announced the appointment of a special investigator to take charge of the murder investigation. Jack nearly spit out his beer when the chief introduced Inspector Terrence Dolan.

Terry wore a crisp white shirt, rep tie, and blue suit. He was the picture of no nonsense law and order. His eyes matched the color of his jacket and he focused them directly on the cameras and ran through what the police had learned so far. It didn't sound like much. The victim's name. Her address. A vague time of death. And an even vaguer description of the cause. The reporters went into a frenzy, jockeying for position to ask questions, but Terry proved to be as skillful at dodging them as he was landing bull's-eyes at the shooting range.

"San Francisco Police Department serves justice and justice will be served. You have my word," he said in closing. Jack was sure that would soon be Terry's tag line.

Wonder Boy was at his usual place behind the bar. He pressed the clicker when the station switched to the studio for the hair-sprayed talking heads. "You went to s-s-school with Terry Dolan, right?" he said to Jack.

"Saint Joe's. It was a long time ago."

"I think Katie's better off with you."

"That makes two of us."

"Terry is a s-s-smart cop though. You better watch your back."

Jack stiffened. "What makes you say that?"

"Word is he has the cops on the beat asking about you, trying to hang s-s-something on you."

"Because of Katie. He's been doing that since we got home from Kathmandu."

Wonder Boy shook his head as he dried a glass. "Doing it more than before. Watch yours-s-self."

JACK WORKED the streets for a while, checking in with a network of snitches and small-time grifters. No one knew anything more about the murder investigation than what had been on TV, but a couple of the skells Jack spoke with confirmed what Wonder Boy said. Terry Dolan had a bigger hard-on for him than usual.

He stopped at Umbria and picked up a takeout order of parmigiana di melanzane and another of gnocchi along with a side of capaccio di salmone. It was dark by the time he got home and when he opened the front door, he saw Brad sitting at the dining table, wearing one of Katie's kimonos and cradling a goblet of white wine. There was an open bottle of Pinot Grigio within easy reach. Katie was buzzing around him with a Q-tip and a tube of organic first aid ointment.

"Hold still," she said. "Hold still."

"What happened to you?" Jack asked, tossing Brad a softball to see if he was going to play along or play the blame game.

Katie's expression swung from concern to anger when she saw Jack. "Look what they did to my little brother. It's all your fault for leaving him in Chinatown."

Jack ignored her. "What happened, Brad?"

"Ouch." Brad shrugged away from his sister's ministrations. "Some guys jumped me." He squared his shoulders and tried to look tough despite wearing a woman's pink and jade robe. "You think I look bad; you should see the others guys. There were three or four of them. I kicked their asses."

Katie clucked and dabbed a scrape on his chin with the stinky balm.

Jack nodded at the kimono. It was 100 percent silk and hand embroidered. He had given it to Katie for her birthday. A present from a fell-off-a-truck distributor he knew. "They take your clothes along with your wallet?"

Brad went for indignant. "I had to throw them away. They were covered in blood. Their blood. God knows what viruses those crackheads have." He shivered. As shivers went, it was pretty good. It even made the Pinot Grigio in his goblet swirl.

"What did you do? Steal an Anything Helps, God Bless sign and walk across town holding it in front of your junk?"

Katie shot Jack a glare. "How can you joke about this? Brad might have a concussion. We need to take him to the ER."

Jack put the takeout cartons on the counter. "What about it, Brad? The docs got to report every banged-up head they see. Doesn't matter if you got it playing football or fell out of bed."

Brad sniffed. "I'll be okay."

"Then I'm going to put some special ointment on those cuts so they don't scar," Katie said. "I have a jar of anti-wrinkle cream made of cotton thistle extract and calf butter in the bathroom."

As soon as she left, Jack said, "Jimmie let you go, huh? Drove you here, dropped you off?"

"What are you talking about?" Brad ratcheted up his indignation to righteous. "He was going to murder me. Throw me off his boat. I escaped."

"You escaped from the Fangs." Jack didn't bother hiding his disbelief. "Okay, how?"

"How isn't important. What is, I'm free."

"No, why Jimmie let you go is what matters."

"I told you already, I escaped. They had me locked in this tiny little closet. It was filthy. Disgusting. I'll never eat Chinese again in my life."

"Then how did you get out?"

Brad started whining. "You suck. You left me there to die. You could've traded your fat friend for me but you didn't. And I'm family too. I'm going to tell Katie."

"And I'm going to hang you out my window for dragging me into this. Now tell me the truth. Why did Jimmie let you go? What did you give him?"

"Nothing. There was this old man who brought me food. He looked to be about a hundred and his right eye dripped. One time he forgot to lock the door and so I just walked away. I mean, so what if they caught me? What did I have to lose?"

"Why did you come here?"

"Where else was I going to go? It's not safe at my apartment anymore. It's not safe for me anywhere. I heard about Mrs. Huntington. You got to protect me, get me out of here. Buy me a ticket to Puerto Vallarta or Tahiti. It doesn't have to be first class. Business will do."

"Why the sudden need to run? You know who killed Mai?"

"No. Why would I?"

"Who do you think did it?"

"It could've been anybody. Mr. Huntington. Cutler. The Fangs. That Jimmie's a killer. Are you going to help me get out of here or not? I need you to buy me a plane ticket. Pay for a hotel room."

"You haven't answered me yet. Why did Jimmie let you go?"

"He didn't. I escaped."

"You don't escape from a guy like Jimmie Fang." Jack took a breath. "Ruddy Face, uh, Cutler, is looking for you. How come?"

"How should I know? Why? What did he say?"

"My guess is his boss is worried you were shooting your mouth off about the chips."

Brad screeched. "I wouldn't do that. I didn't tell anybody."

"What about Hark and me? Jimmie and his dad?"

Brad buried his face in his hands and started to rock. "Oh my God, I got to get out of here. They're going to kill me. You got to help me." He started to shiver, this time for real.

"You're not going anywhere. At least not until I find out why Jimmie let you go."

"That crazy gangster is so mean. You should hear how he talked to me. Called me stupid. And he didn't even go to college. At least I put in two years at City—well, a semester and a half."

"What did Jimmie and his old man say when you told them Huntington had their chips? Were they surprised?"

"Jimmie didn't say anything. It was like he already knew or didn't care. He just ordered those creeps to rip my clothes off and hang me upside down. They spit on me and threw me in a room and tried to poison me with rotten won tons." He continued rocking. "I got to get out of here. I need to get far away."

"Jimmie let you go and if he wants to take you back, he will. It doesn't matter how far you run because he'll find you."

Then Jack's phone buzzed. He didn't have to guess who it was. "Hello, Jimmie. You finally do the math and figured keeping Brad was eating into your overhead? Outsourced him to me for jailing along with finding your chips?"

"Your brother has very bad manners," Jimmie said. "He relieved himself in the corner. He's not here twenty-four hours and he starts scratching days off on the wall. Now we have to spackle and paint. Fang is very angry."

"Brother. In. Law. Tell your old man I'll buy him a can of semigloss." Jack let it hang a few moments. "I told him you'll come collect him if he doesn't help me find what you're looking for, but he doesn't know a thing"

"What have you found out so far?"

"Nothing I care to say on the phone."

"Ah, because of what happened last night. I saw it on TV. A rich woman murdered in her own home. These are troubling times we live in."

"You sound all broken up, especially considering who her husband is."

"You'll be all broken up too if you don't find our chips."

"Fair enough. I have kicked over a couple of rocks, but it's the kind of information best told in person."

Jack heard lovebirds chirping in the background. He pictured Jimmie's apartment. He probably had a gilt birdcage lined with pages cut out of *Vogue*.

Jimmie didn't respond right away. Finally he said, "Come meet me at my club."

"Forget it. I'm not going to paint some room Brad messed up," Jack said.

Jimmie exhaled loudly. "I said my club, not Fang's."

Jack filed away Jimmie's frustration. "Okay. Your club. What's the address?"

Jimmie gave him a number on Hayes Street. "It's very upscale, very fashionable, so find something in your closet from the last decade. You dress like shit."

The phone went dead just as Katie came back with a handful of cotton balls and a jar of ointment. She gave Jack a worried smile. "Can you run down to Whole Foods and pick up some carrot juice? Please? Some fresh beets too. Brad's going to need a strong dose of beta-carotenes."

"That's not all he's going to need," Jack said.

14

Jack drove by city hall, thinking every dime spent rehabbing it was worth it. The great granite building was testament to San Francisco's anything-goes politics and the nearby symphony hall and opera house were proof that the city kept the good times rolling even during recessions and earthquakes. Best of all, the money kept rolling in. It was a great town for his line of work.

When he came to Jimmie's club, Jack circled the block a few times to see who might be waiting in the wings. The little gangster attracted cops and rivals like a porch light draws flying insects, and Jack always wanted to know what kind of bug spray he was going to need before walking into a place.

Nothing caught his eye so he parked the Prius. There was no sign on the door, no flashing neon in the window, just a red velvet rope strung across the sidewalk. A crowd of hopefuls were trying to impress a shaved-head gorilla. He was wearing a headset and a black suit two sizes too small.

Jack walked past. The building housed dentists and doctors by day. An after-hours private elevator whisked him to the top floor. He stepped into a vestibule. A woman wearing six-inch-high heels and a man with hair resembling a flocked Christmas tree smiled pleasantly.

"May we help you?" they said in unison.

Jack gave his name. "I'm Jimmie's long lost cousin."

Their smiles didn't budge but he figured the room had more cameras trained on it than the changing rooms at Bloomie's. Sure enough, a solid wall swished open. The blare of techno rolled toward him. It picked him up and swept him into an overheated room. It was jammed with sweaty dancers who were gyrating under a 1970s-era disco ball, a decade when even jazz had the creative equivalent of a manic depression.

A cocktail waitress sheathed in a dress the size and color of a Band-Aid slithered through the crowd. "This way," she crooned.

Jimmie was seated on a white leather couch in the rear. A skinny guy in tight white leather pants curled next to him. His leopard skin vest and the purple streak in his hair kept him from being mistaken for the armrest.

Jack hooked his thumb at the dance floor. "Trying to keep things the way they used to be, Jimmie?"

"If fashion has taught me anything, it's wait long enough and even wide ties will come back in style." The dapper mobster wrinkled his nose at Jack's clothes. "There's still hope for you."

"I wouldn't bet on bell-bottoms."

Jimmie snapped his fingers. The color on his pinky nail matched the streak in his seatmate's hair. The cocktail server leaned forward. She was no more flexible than a mannequin.

"Great walls," Jimmie said and then patted the couch. "Sit down, Jack. What have you found under those rocks?"

Jack took a seat. The skinny guy in the leather pants bared his canines and snarled.

"He reminds me of a bichon frise ," Jack said. "I hope he's house broken."

Jimmie smiled and stroked the skinny guy's head. "Don't worry, Ronny doesn't bite."

"So long as he doesn't start humping my leg."

"Be kind," Jimmie said. "Now tell me what you know."

"You already knew Sinclair Huntington had your chips when Brad walked through your door."

"What makes you say that?"

"You did. Just now. You've always had the same tell. You twitch your pinky. The one with the purple nail."

Jimmie smiled. "Aren't you the clever one?"

"You knew Huntington had the chips but you don't know which boat they're coming in on. So last night, you went to ask him. Only he wasn't there. But his wife was. You or your lapdog here got a little too worked up while asking her questions, and the next thing she winds up dead. Now you have to start putting distance between you and the murder and clean up loose ends. That's why you let Brad go."

Jimmie laughed. "You watch too many old Jet Li movies. Not only that, you're starting to sound like your chum Terry Dolan. My, isn't he getting all the press?"

"Tell me how I'm wrong," Jack said.

Jimmie scratched Ronny's head. He all but rolled over and put his paws in the air. "Do you think I'd really take on Sinclair Huntington directly?" Jimmie said. "His billions have made him untouchable. He's an iron man. Even the president calls him for advice. Times have changed with these high-tech and hedge fund robber barons running things. It's not the old days."

"Is that why you asked me to do your dirty work? If I succeed, your gamble pays off. If I don't, well, cannon fodder's cheap."

Jimmie smiled, neither confirming nor denying Jack's theory. The waitress returned with the drinks. The glasses were the size of goldfish bowls. All that was missing was a sunken ship and bubbling treasure chest.

"What's in it?" Jack asked.

"Vodka, Baileys, milk, cola, and sambuca," she answered.

"They're divine," Jimmie said and started sucking on the straw. His cheeks puckered deep enough to hide a golf ball.

Jack took a sip. He hoped there was a bottle of aspirin in the Prius. He debated asking Jimmie if he knew Huntington was bringing in the chips as a way to build a business on the side. He decided not to. One way or the other, Jimmie would lie. Besides, it was a card Jack could always play later.

He tried another tack. "Huntington knew all along you had Brad. His crew picked me up and made a show of looking for him. Threatened to do whatever it took to find him. It was all a misdirect. Added smokescreen to cover what's really going on."

Jimmie cocked his head. "What makes you think that?"

"Logic. They don't call it the Information Age for nothing. Huntington all but pioneered it. He traffics in every form of knowledge there is, from snitch to digital. The money has always been in content long before they invented the web. Nothing happens in this city without Huntington's knowledge. The minute Brad walked into your joint Huntington got a call. Probably from someone working for you."

When Jimmie didn't blink, Jack thought maybe he was on to something. Jimmie and Huntington had a lot in common. They were both greedy, both cutthroat, and both operated as if they were above the law. Business partnerships had been founded on a lot shakier common ground.

"I think you're playing me," Jack said. "You and Huntington have been in it together from the start. Somehow you got hold of some computer whizbangs who came up with a faster, smarter self-healing chip set. Getting them manufactured was easy enough. Fab plants are as common in Shenzhen as rainbow flags during Pride Week. The only thing missing were the distribution channels. Something Huntington already has in place. So you guys cut a deal. You make them and he brings them in. But something happened and now he's not playing nice. My guess is he did an end run around your engineers and paid them more, or his own wizards found a way to clone your chips."

Jack swished the straw around in the fishbowl cocktail. "How am I doing so far?"

Jimmie's face tightened and the lapdog growled. "Who's paying you to think?" Jimmie said. "Find my chips or I come collect your brother."

"Everything's changed," Jack said. "There's a murder investigation now. The cops are bound to link it to the chips."

"They're not that bright," Jimmie said.

"But Terry Dolan is."

Jimmie smiled. "That's your problem."

Jack sipped the cocktail and then spit it back into the glass. He waved his hand at the dance floor. "This is some place you've built here. The line waiting to get in is longer than those at the bathrooms during the seventh inning stretch at AT&T Park. The cover, the minimum, the thermostat cranked to eighty degrees to make people thirsty, the markup on the booze. You're doing well for yourself. Your old man must be proud."

"Fang is old school." Jimmie's lips curled as he spoke.

"You haven't had dear old dad over? Show him what you're made of?"

The lapdog started growling again. Jimmie stroked his muzzle. "I told you, Fang is old school. Times have changed."

"It's Jimmie time, huh?"

The triad heir apparent shrugged. The shoulders of his sharkskin suit were as padded as the 49er D-line.

"That go for the microchips?" Jack said. "It's a Jimmie play not Fang's?"

"I don't know what you mean."

"The son also rises. You were banking on those chips to fund a whole new enterprise: moving the triad into the twenty-first century with or without your father."

Jimmie straightened the lapels of his dark suit jacket. "You've been talking gibberish since you got here. All theories, no facts. You still haven't given me any information I can use. Quit fishing and start hunting. You're wasting my time and you're running out of yours. I'm going to reclaim your brother-in-law and take him for a cruise on my Pearl 60." He showed his shark grin again and the bichon frise began to pant. "And, McCoul? There's plenty of room for you on the fantail."

Jack pushed away the disgusting drink. "You want facts? The chips are on a boat. The boat is in the bay. I'll find which one before they make land."

"Aren't you forgetting the most important thing?" Jimmie said. "And give the boat's name to me, no one else."

Jack got up.

"But you haven't finished your great wall," Jimmie said in a voice as sugary as the cocktail.

Jack nodded toward the skinny guy in the white leather pants. "Give it to him. He looks thirsty, all that panting."

One of the worst kinds of bugs scuttled out of the shadows as Jack fished for his car keys.

"I knew you had something going on," Brix said, clamping his hand on Jack's wrist. "And what do you know? It's with Jimmie Fang. I told you, you owe me an opportunity for the time I spent at Soledad. What's the play? What's my end?"

Jack shrugged him off. "I was there for a nightcap. I had it and I'm going home."

"Next you're going to tell me you and Jimmie are going steady, taking evening cruises on his boat, standing on the deck, and drinking champagne while he tosses another triad's soldier overboard. Quit lying to me."

"You've been away too long. You're forgetting something. The only time Jimmie and his old man take on partners are when they need a foursome for golf."

"Don't lie to me. I was in the club checking out the action. Five years is a long time." He mimed humping. "You and Jimmie were as close as Siamese twins. What were you talking about?"

"What to do about his bouncers. They're obviously slipping, letting you in."

Brix made a grab for his wrist again but Jack twisted out of reach. "I hate the way you talk, McCoul. I've had a lot of time to think about how much I hate it."

"Get lost. I got nothing for you."

The ex-con put his hand in the pocket of his zippered Windbreaker to show he was packing. "I ought to shut your mouth right now," he said with a sneer.

Jack adjusted the Prius's key fob in his hand and then remembered there was no key blade he could use as a weapon. He placed his thumb over the alarm button, hoping the shriek would throw Brix's aim off if he couldn't talk his way out of it.

"Do that, and they'll take you straight to the row."

Brix's laugh was a hiss that came out both sides of his mouth. "Cops would have to pin it on me and they're not so good at pinning. Down on the farm? A guy could get away with anything under their noses, including dealing with rats. Didn't matter if a guy was locked in his cell or out in the field. Shank the rat in the chow line or hit it with a hoe. Trust me, it happens and no one's the wiser."

Jack stifled a grimace. "I told you I don't have a play. At least not now. I'm working on a couple of things but nothing's definite. You know how it is. You cast around; you see who bites. I get something, I'll let you know."

Brix kept his hand in his pocket, but started nodding. "That's more like it. I knew you'd come around. Finding us an opportunity. That's all I've been asking for. It's what you owe me."

"You got to be patient. These things take time. You rush it, you flush it."

"I've been waiting five years, McCoul. I don't call that rushing. Go get something and get it fast. I'm done waiting."

Jack shrugged. "I'll work something out; I'll be in touch. How do I find you?"

"You don't. I find you. I know where you live. I know all about you and your family."

Jack opened the Prius's door and got in. He pressed the ignition. The hybrid was so quiet the turning over of the engine didn't make a sound. He lowered the window. "Next time you want to talk to me, use the phone. Don't be seen in public with me or they'll bust us both for associating. Don't come up behind me again. Ever." He slipped the car into drive but kept his foot on the brake. "And don't ever come around where I live. I see you there and I'll call it in myself."

Then he touched the accelerator and glided silently into the night.

15

Jack got a full ride to San Francisco State to play baseball. When he wasn't on the diamond, he attended a few classes. His favorite was theater. It prepared him for his career. Actors and grifters were cut from the same cloth. Both took on a role and used a stage to get people to think they knew who the character was and what he was going to do next. A catch in the voice, a hitch in the gait, a furtive glance of the eyes. These were Jack's tools to make people believe whatever he wanted them to believe.

Baseball, acting, grifting—they all made Jack feel alive. When the game was on the line, be it on the field, the stage or the street, it felt almost as good as making love with Katie. The high got his heart racing, his muscles pumping and all his senses working together, alert to the tiniest detail. Afterward, everything was still going full speed ahead, and he always had to find a way to dial the adrenaline down.

He was feeling that way as he steered the Prius down the quiet streets. Brix had pulled a gun on him, but he handled himself and got out of there without taking a bullet. Jack knew better than to go home right then. Seeing Brad asleep on his couch wouldn't be good for anybody—not him, not Katie, and especially not Brad. Jack needed a release and he needed it now, so he turned the wheel and drove to the Avenues.

Four bars later he found his sister's husband playing eight ball in an Irish pub that served Korean barbeque. Jack shouldered his way through the crowded bar. Derrick was in the far corner, downing more shots of whisky than pool balls as he ranted about the many ways the city's professional sports teams were being screwed out of their due. Derrick's verbal assault was nothing new. He had always been the self-proclaimed expert, the most obnoxious fan in the stadium, and the first to start a brawl whenever someone wearing Dodger blue happened by. If one of Derrick's beloved teams lost, it was Meaghan who bore the brunt of his frustration.

Jack counted three buddies with his brother-in-law. One was too drunk to stand without using a cue for a crutch. Another looked like the type who'd always find a way to be in the bathroom when a check got served or a fight got started. But the third guy was different. He was built like he could handle himself drunk or sober. When he went to the bar to order another round, Jack walked over to the pool table and placed four quarters on the rail.

Derrick tightened his grip on his cue. "Jesus, Jack. What the fuck?"

"It's your table; that means it's your break," he said.

Derrick shook his head. "Come on, man. What the fuck? You come here to bust my balls? Whatever Meaghan told you isn't true. I swear it. I haven't touched her. Jack, there's something you got to know, and I'm sorry to tell you, but your sister's a stone-cold bitch."

Jack crouched and pulled the rack from beneath the table and then fitted in the balls. He slid the wooden triangle back and forth to line them up and then pulled it free. "I'm here to shoot some pool. You going to break or give up the table?"

Derrick grabbed a mug off a nearby table, took a long gulp, and shook his head as the Guinness poured down his throat. He grabbed his cue, chalked it, and broke. The cue ball smacked the head ball straight on. There was a loud crack and a lot of rolling and clicking, but not a single ball found a pocket.

Jack didn't say a word. He went to the cue rack, checked the numbers and the tips, and selected one that wasn't cracked. Then he lined up his shot and proceeded to drop four solids in a row, calling each pocket as he did.

Before he made his fifth shot, he eyed Derrick. "I dropped by Meaghan's. The place is a mess."

Derrick shrugged. "She's a lousy housekeeper and her cooking stinks. Your old man raised a princess. I do what I can. Take out the garbage, pick up stuff. But the house, well, that's her nest."

Jack held the cue out. It had a noticeable curve. "She's a mess. And you're a bigger mess. The kids deserve better. You need to get into a program."

"What the fuck you talking about? I don't need a fucking program. I need a fucking job, that's what. The fucking recession was hard on a lot of us. Wasn't like I got any training so I could get one of those fat high-tech jobs. I would've but I had to drop out of school when our first was born. That's the kind of father I am. Hey, I do what I can."

Jack rolled the cue on the flat of his palm until he found the side with the least amount of curve. "You don't get in a program, you don't get a job, then you don't come around the house anymore. You made bad choices in life. It's time to make the right one."

"Who the fuck are you to come in here and bust my balls? I

know what you do. You want to help your sister? Give her some more skrill. It's not like you're paying taxes and can't afford it."

"I told Meaghan she should talk to a lawyer about drawing up papers," Jack said. "She's worried about what the church will say, but I say divorce is the only way to get you to believe what's happening here is real. Consider it an intervention. She gets those papers, you're going to sign them."

"Says who?"

Jack didn't answer. He lined up another shot and dropped it. Two more and he called the eight, banked it off the far rail, curled it around a couple of stripes, and watched it sink. "Make the right choice for a change," he said. "Be a man and do right by your family. You're all grown up. Act like it."

Derrick took another gulp of beer and squeezed the foam from his goatee. "You got some balls coming in here telling me how to run my family. She may be your sister but she's my wife. Those are my kids. I'll treat them any way I want."

"There you go again. Making another bad choice. You can't treat them any way you want."

"Yeah, says who?"

"Protective Services for starters. They find out you raised a hand to them again, they'll throw you in jail. I find out? You won't know until it's already happened."

When Derrick realized people were watching, he stuck out his chest. "Yeah, well, ooh, I'm really scared. Blow me." He made a face and led his audience in a cheer.

Jack waited for the boozy shouts to die. "Let me spell out the right choice for you again. Get yourself in a program. Learn how to manage your anger issues. Quit drinking. Get yourself a real job. And don't go home until you do."

Derrick tried staring Jack down but blinked first. Reinforcements arrived when his burly friend showed up. He cradled three shot glasses. "Who's this asshole?" he asked.

"Meaghan's brother," Derrick said.

"He one of the losers or the so-called hustler?"

Jack laid the pool cue on the table and rolled it back and forth a couple of times. "This one's crooked. I wouldn't try it if I were you."

He pushed past Derrick and the bruiser. He nearly made it to the door before the first shot glass sang past his ear and shattered against the wall. Jack ducked the next, wheeled around, and caught the third as it came hurtling toward him. He zinged it at Derrick's drinking buddy. It nailed him square on the chin and dropped him. Jack reached the table in two strides with the cue in his hands. He had it cocked back ready to swing for the fences.

Derrick whitened and covered his face. "Come on, Jack. What the fuck? Don't. Okay. You got my word. I'll never go around her again."

Jack felt the bat in his grip and saw the fastball coming in hot. His coiled body started to unwind. He threw his hips into it. And then just like that, all the tension he'd been bottling up let go. The release flooded through him like it always did after being on the diamond or the stage or after a play was over, and he'd gotten away with it.

He laid the cue on the table and waggled a finger at Derrick. "That's what I'm talking about. Making the right choice, don't you know?"

16

Katie was making egg white omelets with asparagus and Jack was weighing the pros and cons of rummaging through the refrigerator for some bacon that had cost a pig its life, not a soybean's. In the end, he decided to be content with watching her dance around the kitchen. She flipped the omelet while feeding mangoes, beets, yeast extract, and wheatgrass into a whirring blender.

"He really going to drink that?" Jack asked, hooking his thumb toward the couch where Brad was curled into the fetal position with an afghan tucked under his chin.

"Brad's still very woozy," Katie said over her shoulder. "I'm trying to rebalance his electrolytes to stimulate healing."

"I can think of something else that could use stimulating."

She waved the spatula at him. "Honestly? After last night?"

Jack grinned and then glanced at the *San Francisco Chronicle.* He scrolled through the latest account on Mai's murder. The cops hadn't found anything new, or at least they weren't telling if they had. The big news was the $1 million reward Sinclair Huntington had offered for the capture and conviction of his wife's killer.

"Like to see him pay that off," Jack muttered.

The doorbell rang. Jack started to push away from the table. "Must be one of your students who lives in the building; otherwise, they'd be buzzing us from the street."

Katie switched off the blender. "Stay put, I'll get it."

Jack went back to the rehash of the murder. There was the usual scared talk from the neighbors and a formal statement from the mayor asking the board of supervisors to reconsider a recent vote to cut the police department's budget.

Katie opened the door. "Oh my God, Terry. What are you doing here?"

Inspector Dolan wasn't alone. The blond, blockheaded cop named Carter and the one with the collar mic stood behind.

Terry's eyes seemed to shine even brighter than usual as he stared at Katie. "You look gor..." He caught himself. "Still doing yoga, I see."

"I was making breakfast. Are you boys hungry?"

"Some other time," Terry said, his voice flattening into the same tone he used at the press conference. "We're here on official business."

He sidestepped Katie and walked in. The two uniformed cops followed. "Well, Jack, I assume you know why we're here."

Jack closed the flap on his tablet as deliberately as if he was folding a newspaper, winked at Katie, and then smiled at Terry. "The trouble when you assume something? You make an ass out of you and me."

The detective grimaced. "You're playing word games while a woman lies dead in the morgue." He turned to Katie. "And you could've had an honest marriage."

Katie, her eyes growing wide, said, "What woman?"

Jack stood. "The woman from Pacific Heights. It's all over the news. Her name is Mai Huntington. She was married to the tech mogul Sinclair Huntington."

"What does that have to do with us?"

"Nothing," Jack said. "Terry here is doing his job as head of the investigation. He's running down leads no matter how ridiculous they are because he hasn't found a thing yet. At least not according to the *Chronicle* this morning. I attended the game developer convention gala the other night at Moscone and spoke with the Huntingtons."

"So you don't deny it?" Terry said.

"Why should I? I spoke to lot of people that night."

"How come? You don't work for a tech company."

Jack smiled. "I'm a venture capitalist. Tech's where the smart money is. You should look into a technology job yourself. Bet being a rent-a-cop at Twitter pays a helluva lot more than what you're bringing in, even with all the mandatory overtime."

Terry wore a grimace. "Then you won't have a problem coming to the hall and answering a few questions."

"What do you call what we're doing?"

"I mean a formal questioning."

"Ah, an interrogation. Do you guys still use magazines? My old man used to tell a story about your dad. Turns out, Demon Eamon had a subscription to *Playboy*. Used it for both kinds of whacking."

Terry started forward and the blond, blockheaded cop reached for his Maglite.

Katie stepped in front of them. "Don't you need a warrant or something?"

Jack put his hands on her shoulders and pulled her close. "Don't worry, babe," he said into her ear. "It's just Terry being Terry. Feed Brad his smoothie. Call Hark if you need anything. I'll be back before your omelet falls."

Jack would pay for it when Terry got him into the box at the hall, but some things had to be done. He kissed her long and hard until the spatula slipped from her hand.

DOWN ON THE STREET, a squad car with its lights flashing was parked diagonally in front of the entrance. An unmarked black Crown Vic was pulled in next to it.

"Best thing about being a cop is the double parking, huh, Terry?" Jack said.

"Get in," the detective ordered, opening the rear door to the Crown Vic.

Terry slid behind the wheel and hit the automatic lock button. He drove fast but confidently, one eye focused on the rearview mirror. "You realize what you did to Katie? What you're putting her through? You make me sick." He hit a switch and the siren chirped as he ran a red light.

"Not bad off the line," Jack said. "I read they stopped making the Vic's Police Interceptor model in 2011. How many miles on it? Before too long you'll have to shop around for a new ride. This being San Francisco, the department should consider going green. Try a Prius. Katie's and mine gets fifty-five miles to the gallon. When we have kids, we're going to trade it in for the station wagon model."

Terry grimaced in the rearview mirror. Jack smiled to himself. Interrogation was definitely going to be a bitch now, but that's what he wanted. No matter the game, it was always an advantage to keep the opponent off balance.

THE SAN FRANCISCO Hall of Justice was on Bryant Street. It was as gray and intimidating as a battleship. Besides courtrooms and offices, it held two jails that bunked over two thousand inmates a night. Most hadn't been convicted and were being held for trial. Some had been waiting for months. The police department had ten station houses scattered throughout the city's neighborhoods and while each had an interrogation room and a holding cell, homicide detectives liked to do their questioning at the hall. They'd purposely hit the wrong elevator button while escorting a suspect and get off on a floor housing cellblocks. Then they'd offer a lame excuse about a shortcut and lead the suspect along a hallway lined with metal pens crammed with crims and crazies. The technique worked almost as well as a thick magazine to the back of the head.

Jack was no stranger to the hall, but he'd never been brought in for questioning about a murder before. Terry didn't bother signing him in. He led him through a series of cramped rooms cops used when coming downtown to make a court appearance. It was as transitory as a hostel. Coffee cups and fast food wrappers covered nearly every surface. The computer monitors on the battered desks were last year's model five years ago. Cubbies held gym bags. A greasy mist from dirty socks, kimchi, and Axe aftershave coated everything.

"Grab a chair," Terry said, ushering Jack into a cubicle with a flickering florescent light, a two-way mirror on the wall, and a metal desk carved with initials and gang signs.

Jack sat on a metal office chair with a torn green vinyl seat cover. "What, no forms to sign, no Miranda rights?"

"We won't need them," Terry said, sitting on the edge of the desk. "I'm going to ask questions and you're going to answer them. Then I'm going to tell you the facts of life."

"Sorry, Terry, my old man wasn't good for much but he did give me the talk. If memory serves I was about ten at the time."

"Keep it up and you'll have plenty of time to practice smart mouthing behind bars." Terry glanced at the two-way mirror without moving his head. "How long have you known Mai Huntington?"

"I told you already. I met her at Moscone Center the night of the gamer gala."

"Witnesses say you were acting pretty cozy for having just met. That thing she did with her tongue?"

"I took it to mean she didn't like pimentos. You should see what Katie can do with a—"

Terry slammed his hand down on the top of the desk. "Shut up and answer the questions."

Jack shrugged. "I thought I was."

"Sinclair Huntington said you and his wife were acting like you had something to hide. What was it?"

"Huntington has an overactive imagination. He seems to be the jealous type." Jack let it hang. "Aren't jealous husbands usually the prime suspects when the wife gets shot to death?"

"Who said anything about being shot?"

"I just assumed it given Huntington's marital record." He drew out 'assumed' and then mimed pointing a gun to his head. "My guess is a lot of people you've talked to say he drove his first wife to blow her brains out. Am I right?"

"Shut up. I'm asking the questions here."

"Are you?"

Terry didn't take the bait. "How come when I stopped you at Moscone, you started bad-mouthing Sinclair Huntington?"

Jack turned from Terry to the mirror to make sure the camera was getting it all. "Actually, Inspector Dolan, on the night in question, you called me a parasite. The strange thing is, that's the exact word Huntington had called me a few minutes earlier. Naturally, I wondered if you spoke with him prior to chasing after me. As if he had ordered you to. What I said to you was, 'who are you working for?' And you said, 'the people of San Francisco.' And I said, 'Does that include Sinclair Huntington?' "

Terry smacked the table again. "Quit looking at the mirror. Did Mrs. Huntington call you the day after the gala? Yes or no."

Her caller ID was blocked but Jack figured they had her phone records by now anyway.

"Yes. Mrs. Huntington called me while I was at lunch with my wife. If memory serves, Katie and I shared two dozen oysters on the half shell and a bottle of wine. We had plans to go home and take a nap. You ever eat oysters? They're quite aphrodisiacal."

Terry turned to the mirror and sliced his fingers across his neck. He waited a minute and then stood.

"Is this the point where you go looking for a magazine?" Jack asked, keeping it relaxed but readying his reflexes just in case.

"I don't need a fucking magazine."

"Why, Terry, I've never heard you swear before. Father Bernardus is going to give you ten Hail Marys."

The cop was on him in a flash. He grabbed the front of Jack's shirt and then pulled him out of the chair. Jack let himself go limp rather than resist. If Terry slugged him he'd own him.

"You make me sick," Terry shouted. "You're nothing but a fucking thief, and stealing is the worst crime of all. You rob a person and you steal not only what belongs to them, you steal their time. You lie; you steal their trust. You commit murder; you steal their life and rob their family. And when you commit adultery, you rob a person of their heart."

"Exodus," Jack said. "With a little bit of Romans and Dr. Phil thrown in. Remember? I went to Saint Joe's too."

Terry tightened his grip on Jack's shirtfront and tried lifting him off the ground. "You're a thief, Jack. You stole Katie from me, and now, goddamnit, I'm going to put you away for robbing Mai Huntington of her life. I got it all. You were there."

"That's what you still don't get. You blame me for Katie, but that's thinking she's no different than a wristwatch. You can't steal love. It's something you give."

The detective's face turned the color of blood. "I was going to marry her until you came along."

"There you go again. It's not 'I was going to;' it's 'we were going to.' If Katie had loved you she would've married you. I couldn't have gotten in the way of that. No one could've."

Terry drove Jack backward, knocking over the metal chair and then slamming him into the wall. "You've always been a thief. And the sick thing is? You cheat people into liking you for it. At the United Irish potlucks, after you'd pull one of your shenanigans? The fathers would laugh and clap your dad on the back. And the mothers, you had them fooled too. They called you heartache and heartbreak all rolled into one."

Jack coughed. The body slam knocked the wind out of him. Terry didn't stop. "But the worst of it? You cheated me out of my honor. Made me do something unforgiveable, pulling my weapon that night at Katie's apartment. You made me go against everything I believe in, stand for, lead my life by. An oath that keeps people like me from sinking into the slime with people like you."

Jack, wheezing some, said, "Look at your precious oath now. You know I didn't kill Mai Huntington. By now you've already run down my whereabouts. The pubs in the Avenues where I was searching for Meaghan's deadbeat husband. The cabbie who gave me a ride home? You talked to him. Showed him my photograph. And what did he tell you? Halfway there I told him I only had a few bucks on me and he better let me out. You canvassed the neighborhood. You talked to the bartender on Union Street. You know Hark came to give me a lift, that we had a nightcap."

Jack caught his breath. "So get your hands off me before you become a bigger hypocrite than you already are. Beat me, book me, or let me go because we both know what this is really about. And it's not Mai Huntington."

Terry's rage began to cool. He had bitten his bottom lip. Droplets of blood were bubbling on it. "This investigation is far from over. As far I'm concerned you're still my prime."

He let go of Jack's shirt, wheeled around, and went to the door. As soon as he pulled it open, the blond blockheaded cop rushed in.

"You need help, Inspector?"

Terry pushed by him. "McCoul's free to go. For now."

Jack started to follow but the uniformed cop blocked his way. "I watched it all from in there," Carter said, pointing at the mirror. "I was rooting for him to level your ass."

Jack moved to step around him. "Sorry to disappoint. You need kicks? Try watching the UFC channel."

Carter sucker punched him in the kidneys. "You're going down. I guaranfuckingtee it."

17

When Jack was at St. Joseph's, Father Bernardus was always preaching about the evils of relying on superstition. He used to say there was a big difference between rubbing a St. Christopher medal and carrying animal figurines around, but Jack didn't believe it for a minute. Everyone he knew had a lucky charm, Jack included. It was the reason he had a shamrock inked in green on his shoulder.

Sinclair Huntington was no different. Jack was sure of it. Anybody who wore solid gold double-8 cuff links wasn't about to load $100 million worth of smart chips into a metal box and send it bobbing across the Pacific without doing the numerological equivalent of kissing a horseshoe. Jack figured Huntington had worked lucky eights into the container's serial shipping container code in some fashion or another. All he needed was the name of the ship to find it.

Jack was hunkered at the dining table, the room lit only by the glow of the tablet's screen so as not to wake Brad, who had crashed out on the pullout sofa. Not that a 6.3 on the Richter scale could have shaken him into consciousness. He had diluted his smoothie with a pint of Goose and chased down a handful of muscle relaxants. Jack searched the AIS site and started listing the names associated with all the blinking arrows representing ships bound for the Oakland docks. It was the Match.com of shipping and there were dozens to sift through, but none were jumping out with a come-hither smile and a "sexy princess seeks handsome hunk" headline saying, "choose me, choose me."

Katie was asleep when Jack got home so he was surprised when she tiptoed from their bedroom, stooped behind him, and put her arms around his neck. She was wearing a kimono and he hoped it wasn't the one she lent Brad.

"I've been worried sick about you," she said.

"Sorry. Had some things to do, people to see after I finished at the hall."

"Is everything okay?"

"Right as rain, don't you know?"

Katie pressed against him. He could feel her breasts. "I'm sorry if Terry was tough on you because of me. I'd hoped he was over it by now."

Jack didn't say anything. Katie wasn't the kind of woman men got over. Ever. She had that natural ability to make Jack feel better about himself, give his life meaning as well as a sense of purpose. And he figured Terry thought the same thing; it was why he was fighting so hard to win her back.

Jack kept following the boat icons blinking across the screen. Katie pressed harder against him and started nibbling his ear. "What are you doing?"

"Looking for a ship."

"Why? Are you going somewhere?"

"Not without you."

"What's it called?"

"Ship of Fools."

Katie laughed. It was the best laugh in the world, pure and free and unabashed. The kind of laugh that was so contagious, so liberating, it could split Jack's sides and bring tears to his eyes. He loved her laugh. Loved hearing it, especially when she was pressing her breasts against him and tenderizing his ear with her lips.

She loosened an arm and tapped the screen. "How about this one? *Northern Lights*. That's a pretty name."

"Wrong kind. That's an oil tanker from Alaska."

"What makes this boat so important you have to find it in the middle of the night instead of coming to bed? Does it have to do with the murder Terry is trying to solve?"

Jack ached to tell her the truth—that Terry was trying to pin the murder on him. After he left the hall, Jack did some digging. A snitch confirmed that Terry kept the lab rats at the crime scene bagging and tagging evidence. The murder book was growing thicker by the minute. Beat cops were under orders to show Jack McCoul's photograph to their network of informants; everyone knew about the $1 million reward. As Jack made the round of haunts, seeking information, his gut told him he was being followed. He figured Terry was having him tailed, and it added to the weight of the great big bull's-eye on his back.

His last stop before coming home had been the Pier Inn. Hark joined him there. Jack shared what he'd learned. Hark agreed they couldn't leave solving the crime up to Terry. Jack's livelihood always depended on his willingness to gamble, but this was one game he wasn't about to risk to chance. He needed to prove who killed Mai, and he was sure the chips were the key. He not only needed luck to locate the ship, he needed help.

Jack turned from the tablet's screen and faced Katie. "It's true confession time, babe. "I wasn't completely upfront about Brad and Chinatown. His being there has to do with a scam."

Before he could get another word out, Katie recoiled and pushed him away. The sleepy, sexy smile on her lips quickly turned upside down. "You promised you'd quit," she said. "And now you've dragged my brother into something illegal." Revulsion filled her beautiful eyes. "Don't tell me you have anything to do with that murder? Oh my god."

Jack took hold of her wrists and placed his thumbs on a spot she had showed him was connected to a person's whatever it's called that calmed them down. "Just hear me out," he said. And so he told her. The whole story.

When he was through, Katie threw her arms around him again. "You're the best brother-in-law in the world. You're so brave. I always knew you loved Brad." Jack bit his tongue. Katie's expression grew serious. "So what can I do to help?"

Jack pointed at the tablet's screen. "I need to find a shipping container that holds the chips, but I don't know which ship. It could be any one of these."

Katie gave him another ear nibble. "Okay, let's find it and then we can go to bed. It should be easy enough." She pressed her face against his so they were looking at the screen cheek to cheek. "Let's see. You don't know the boat's name. You don't know where it's coming from. You don't know when it's going to dock. Do you at least know where it's going?"

"Port of Oakland."

"Obvi. Where else would it go? You already said it's not a tanker. Those all go to the refinery terminals in Richmond. And only cruise ships dock here in the city. I meant, where are they going to take the container once it's off the ship? If you knew that, you could backtrack it."

"What do you mean?"

"It's like when I plan our vacations. I begin with the finish and work backward. Let's say we want to go to a sunny beach in the Caribbean. Remember that time on St. Croix? I loved that. Topless yoga on the beach. Smoothies made with fresh pineapple, banana, and papaya. That fantastic room we had with the view of the ocean from the most comfortable bed in the world."

She stared off dreamily. “Anyway, next I choose the island. And then the hotel. And then the flight. And then the BART ride to SFO. Finish to start.”

He’d been going about it all wrong. There were fewer old computer chip manufacturing plants around than ships. Jack spun around and pulled her onto his lap. “Brilliant. Why didn’t I think of that?”

She tapped her head. “Women’s intuition. We see the big picture, the whole story. There’s a saber-toothed tiger outside the cave and all a man sees is danger. But the cave woman sees food for her children, fur for a blanket, whiskers for thread, and claws for tools. Not that I’d hurt a tiger, of course.”

“Roar,” he said.

They started kissing and Katie said, “So can we go to bed now?”

Jack carried her across the loft and kicked the door closed behind them. They fell onto the bed. Fell like they were going over a waterfall, laughing and shrieking the whole wild ride down.

18

The sun was shining and the traffic was light on 101 South. If it weren't for Brad slumped in the passenger seat, Jack would've called it the start to a beautiful day.

"Why did you get me up so early?" Brad whined. "It's still dawn."

"In Hawaii. You're sleeping your life away."

"Thanks, Dad. I already told you I don't know where Mr. Huntington's sending the chips. All Cutler told me it was a closed manufacturing plant somewhere in Silicon Valley. It could be anywhere. Mountain View. Cupertino. San Jose." He spit the cities out like they were the names of hemorrhagic fevers. "Did you bring any meds with you? I'm really hurting here. Do I need to remind you I received serious injuries at the hands of that psychopath you left me with?"

"Concentrate on everything Ruddy Face talked about. How long would it take to haul them from Oakland to the plant? What did the place look like? What bars and restaurants were nearby? Strip joints. Cardrooms."

Brad groaned. "I need something to kill the pain. I'm lucky to remember my own name after what Jimmie did to me. My head is pounding. Pounding. Katie's sure I have a concussion."

"I'll be happy to drop you off at the hospital once we find the plant."

"And have them report me? No way. No cops. They all work for Mr. Huntington."

"What makes you say that?"

"They're always around. The entire force is moonlighting for him. Providing security at his big conferences, the dinner parties at his mansion, his sailing races."

Jack thought of Terry Dolan. Even altar boys could fall from grace.

Brad started moaning again. "I got to have something that will knock me out until this whole nightmare is over."

"You'll be able to wake up a lot sooner if you help me find where they're taking the chips."

"Why do you need me anyway? Just start calling trucking companies and say you work for Mr. Huntington. Fake them into telling you when and where they're picking up the container."

Jack rejected it. Huntington's name wouldn't be associated in any way with the container and there were dozens of drayage outfits he'd have to dial and dance with.

"The shipment is coming in off the books. Mai said she couldn't find any record of it. Huntington must have set up a dummy shell and layered it under all sorts of other shells he can disavow. But if I can nail down the plant's address, then I can search online public records for a fictitious business name registration. I need that first."

"It's too much work," Brad whined. "It's too hard."

"So's staying alive. There's already been one murder. You want to keep out of Huntington and Jimmie's clutches, not to mention Terry Dolan? Then you better start pitching in. Come on, think. Someone had to have said something."

They passed SFO and started down the peninsula. Realtors had leveraged this area for the high-tech industry professionals who had a penchant for passing out stock options like Halloween candy. Soon, plain vanilla three bedroom suburban ranch houses sold for $2 million and more. Jack's gut told him the manufacturing plant had to be somewhere in the heart of Silicon Valley. Before leaving he had done some mapping. Ground zero for former silicon fabrication plants was a five-mile stretch between Sunnyvale and Santa Clara.

Back in the day, landing a job at Intel or National Semi was the equivalent of getting a free lifetime pass to the Magic Kingdom. It gave instant access to the middle class and beyond. The party rolled on for years until someone remembered that toys and transistor radios used to be made in America too. Then faster than you could say microprocessor, most of the chip manufacturers and the jobs that went with them took the same route as heavy industry did. They sailed off to places like India, Malaysia, and China.

Brad started moaning. "I'm starving. I haven't eaten any real food for days. I need a burger. There's an In-N-Out up ahead."

"How do you know that?"

"Cutler told me."

"He did, huh? How well do you know him?"

"Good enough to know he's a total animal. Don't ever play cards with him. He can't tell the difference between a gentleman's bet and a real one."

"Meaning you lost to him and then tried saying it was all a joke. You're lucky he doesn't use you as an anchor. Is that why he was so hot to find you? It wasn't about the chips; it's about your chits."

"I don't owe Cutler a cent. Well, not really. I mean, it was a mix-up."

"I don't want to hear it. I want to know where this plant is. What else did Ruddy Face say?"

Brad whined. "I told you. I don't know. I'm starving. Take me to the In-N-Out. Please?"

Jack blew out some air. "All he told you was he had lunch there, that it?"

"Uh-huh. He said he had a strawberry shake with his Double-Double. He usually has a chocolate but they messed up the order. Too many strawberries, not enough chocolates."

"So, he didn't eat alone? Did he say who he was with?"

"I think a lot better with food in my stomach. I'm about to pass out. Really."

"And I'm about to push you out of the car. Really. Tell me more about this In-N-Out. What else did he say?"

"Nothing. Cutler just mentioned the strawberry shake and complained about there being a long line in the drive-thru. So what? There always is."

"Meaning he did takeout. Ruddy's a gofer. Whoever he was retrieving food for had to be close by. Nobody likes a cold burger and a warm shake."

Jack took the next off-ramp and swung into a parking lot. A quick check on his phone pinpointed the In-N-Out. Three of the shuttered fab plants he'd mapped earlier were within a mile radius.

Brad was scarfing a Double-Double as they sat parked near the entrance to a driveway that lead into a business park. The first two plants had been busts. One had been converted into a solar panel manufacturer and the other was now a Tesla dealership. Jack called this one Lazarus. He could see down the drive to a parking lot at the side of the building. Pickups and panel vans crowded the first row of stalls. A steady flow of carpenters, electricians, and machinists came and went.

"I got to use the bathroom," Brad said.

"Sit tight and wiggle your toes. I'm going to take a look around. Won't be a minute," Jack said.

He walked down the drive and followed a plumber into the building. The place hummed with activity. Cubicles lined the far side. Each workstation was outfitted with a new flat screen monitor and an electron microscope. Another side was fitted with floor-to-ceiling metal shelves and automated conveyors that connected to a double-wide truck bay. Workers were stacking flats of cardboard boxes and huge bags of antistatic shipping peanuts.

Clear acrylic walls enclosed an enormous clean room that occupied the center of the building. Fluorescent lights gave it an antiseptic glow. An army of technicians assembled machinery and lab equipment. Jack imagined it when it was completed. It would be hopping with workers dressed in bunny suits monitoring silicon wafer sheets moving along the assembly line. He whistled in appreciation. Huntington was not only bringing in the chips from China to pass them off as American-made, he was building the means to produce them wholesale. The Fangs wouldn't be happy.

"Hey, fella, what the fuck you doing in here?" asked a muscular guy with a buzz cut. He wore a private security gray suit and an earpiece. He was walking quickly toward Jack.

Jack grinned. "Name's Steve Apple. Cutler sent me." He stuck out his hand but the guard refused to shake. Jack grinned wider. "I know. My parents were the original geeks. They worshipped Jobs and the Woz. Even owned a Lisa. The only thing they didn't do was buy stock in the company when it went public."

"I don't know any Cutler," the granite-jawed guard said.

Jack cocked his head. "Really? Big guy, sunburned complexion? Anyway, Cutty—that's what all of us who crew on Mr. Huntington's yacht call him—he told me to roll on down and see about a job."

"Nobody's hiring nobody." The guard jerked his thumb toward the open bay. "Move out."

Jack made a show of looking around. "Sure seems like there's plenty of work. I drive forklift when I'm not crewing on Mr. Huntington's yacht. Riders, reachers, walkies, sideloaders. You name it; I can steer it. Cutty said they needed help off-loading a shipping container. If it needs picking and stacking, I'm your man. Never dropped a pallet in my life."

"And I told you I don't know nobody named Cutler. Never heard of nobody named Huntington. Don't know nothing about no boat. And I sure as hell don't know nothing about no container. Now hit the bricks, dickhead. Double-time."

"Gee, sorry. I guess I got the wrong address," Jack said and headed for daylight.

The big guy dogged him the whole way. Jack half expected to be tackled as he neared his car. What he didn't expect was it to be empty.

"Dammit, Brad," he said, not caring what the security guard thought.

Jack fired up the Prius and went in search. Brad either got lost or found a hole to crawl in. The thought of Cutler and the winch monkeys happening by while he was inside the fab plant entered Jack's mind, but he brushed it off. Denial wasn't just for coal companies who refused to believe in climate change. He gave his brother-in-law the benefit of the doubt and stopped at the nearest gas station to check the men's. He even opened the door to a port-a-potty parked in front of a construction site. What he did for love.

19

"You got to let me bomb this ride," Hark said as Jack steered through the Mission District. "I could drop it three inches, put on some twenty-four-inch rims, spray a nice mural on the side."

"Katie would go for a mural but not the rims," Jack said. "Might interfere with the mileage."

Hark pointed at the dashboard display. "That's nearly as big as my widescreen at home. You don't worry about getting distracted and rear-ending someone at a red?"

"Let's me know I'm being eco-friendly, even when I'm not feeling so hospitable."

"Like you are now, *vato*. What's Katie going say when you tell her you lost her punk brother?"

"I'm hoping we find him before it gets to that. She's always been a mother bear when it comes to Brad."

"It's why you like her. Balances you out and appeals to your feminine side."

Jack gave him a sideways glance. "You're on her e-mail list now, aren't you? Don't tell me you've been watching all those links she sends to her clients?"

Hark nodded. "I'm getting tired of channel surfing every night. Besides, some of the stuff she sends is pretty good. In an educational sort of way. Makes me understand why when a low low comes in and asks me to spray a herd of unicorns galloping on the doors of his whip, it's because he's got penis envy issues. It's all about being sensitive to your customers. Says so in my 'Lowrider for Dummies' book."

Jack drove down O'Farrell Street, which was crowded with addicts and streetwalkers.

"Katie's brother lives in the Tenderloin?" Hark asked.

"We're going to turn up a block. Realtors call that stretch the Tendernob now."

"Hundred feet closer to Nob Hill don't make much of a difference," Hark said. "Punk's kinda light and slight to be living in the TL. Doesn't have the 'don't fuck with me' look you need."

"It's all Brad can afford," Jack said. "He's always waiting for the next big score. Brad's one of those guys who waits for his life to start and then realizes at the end he's already lived it."

"He should've gone to the 'Stan like me. Two seconds in the sandbox and you know for sure your life's happening right here and now."

Jack pulled up in front of a six-story purple apartment building. Paint was peeling from the fire escape. "Brad's got a studio on the fifth floor. I'm hoping he's hiding under the bed. Better warn you ahead of time, the elevator doesn't always work and even then, it's usually safer to use the stairs."

Hark was wearing an untucked long-sleeved flannel shirt that was buttoned at the neck. He lifted the tails to show the butt of the Beretta M9 tucked into his waistband. "In case of roaches," he said.

The lobby had old carpeting and a couple of old, sagging couches with a few old, sagging tenants sitting on them. Jack led the way to the staircase.

"Don't use the banister unless you're also packing a bottle of Purell," he said.

Hark was huffing by the time they reached Brad's floor. "Tell Katie to sign me up for one of her gym classes. All that office work I'm doing, I'm out of shape."

"I can see it now," Jack said. "She'll start you on a spin bike wearing skintight shorts, have you eating gluten-free and drinking colonics in no time."

Hark had his hands on his knees. "This getting old shit sucks. I used to be able to hump a sixty-pound rucksack while carrying a twenty-five-pound SAW up and down mountains goats wouldn't climb."

Every other overhead light in the hallway was burned out. Brad's apartment was toward the end. Jack raised a fist and knocked. No answer. He knocked again. A couple of doors on either side opened a crack and then slammed shut.

"Neighborly place," Hark said.

Jack twisted the knob. It was locked. He pulled out his picks and had the door open in under a minute.

"Haven't lost your touch," Hark said.

They went inside. The apartment was wallpapered with photographs cut out of magazines. There were pictures of sports cars, expensive clothes, and famous actresses.

Hark whistled. "Talk about penis envy. Punk's all about unicorns."

"Brad's a dreamer, that's for sure."

Jack toured the room. He pushed open the door to the bathroom and pulled down the Murphy bed.

"Look at this," Hark said. A technology magazine lay open on a wobbly table. It was turned to a spread on self-healing microchips. "Was doing his homework."

"I hope this doesn't mean what I think it means," Jack said.

"Meaning what?"

"Brad was trying to figure out what the chips are worth, what they could bring on the street." Jack grimaced. "He was planning to rip off a few boxes when they were unloading them."

"Those sailor dudes probably found out. It's why they're looking for him. They've probably been tailing you all along and grabbed him while you were checking out the chip plant."

"Could be," Jack said. "I sure have been getting the feeling somebody's been shadowing me wherever I go. I just figured it was the cops."

"Terry," Hark said. "He's his old man's kid, that's for sure. Whenever we had a little dustup over turf in the Mission, Demon Eamon would chase us like a dog after a cat."

Jack nodded. "It's either the cops or Ruddy Face and his crew. Then again, it could be the wild card tagging after me. I've never been in a play yet when there wasn't one."

"Who'd that be?" Hark asked.

"Caspar Brixton. He's out of Soledad now and still blames me."

"Figures. The only thing the dudes I know ever learned in the joint was how to hold a grudge."

Jack nodded. "And Brix graduated top of his class."

"So let's go ask him if he's got Brad."

"Sure, as soon as we rule out the usual suspects."

It took a half hour to drive from the TL to the southwestern-most corner of the city. It took longer to find out that's where Fang was. Jack called Jimmie on his private number but didn't get an answer, not even voice mail. He canvassed the city's bookies and learned Jimmie's dad was playing eighteen on the Ocean Course at the Olympic Club.

"Fang's a member here?" Hark asked as Jack wheeled the

Prius past the walled entrance of the country club. "Since when did the white dudes let people of color in here to do something other than wait on their tables and mow their grass?"

"Hasn't been that long, actually," Jack said. "Women too. It took a lawsuit to change it all. I'll bet you there's more golf clubs in a player's bag than African American, Asian American, and Latino members here."

"That ain't right," Hark said.

The fog had settled thickly over the heavily forested course perched alongside the Pacific. Jack parked and made straight for the pro shop's garage. A jackson to the kid cleaning carts got them a freshly charged one and a course map.

"This fast as this thing go?" Hark said as they puttered down a path that ringed a fairway. "Could fix that by dropping in a four-stroke. Paint job could use some cherrying. No reason not to have style when you're chasing a little white ball with a stick."

They caught up to Fang's foursome on the fifteenth, the furthest fairway from the clubhouse. Fang and another player stood over a ball. The other two players reached into their golf bags and pulled out automatic rifles. They pointed them at Jack and Hark.

"It's Jack McCoul," he called to Fang who was taking practice swings with a 5-iron. "I tried calling your son. We need to talk."

Fang was wearing a black golf cap with a white Titleist logo on it and matching sweater and slacks. He lit a Double Happiness and then nodded to the two bodyguards with the ARs. They approached Jack's cart from both sides.

"Hark's carrying," Jack told them. "He's going to put his piece in the basket behind the seat while I talk to your boss, okay?"

Hark didn't look happy as he slowly pulled out his Beretta and placed it down carefully.

Jack walked across the thick, spongy grass. The mist was so

thick he could barely make out the flag marking the hole on the green ahead. Fang stared at him through cigarette smoke. One eye was narrower than the other.

Jack bowed slightly. "I apologize for interrupting your game but my brother-in-law, who you and your son entrusted in my care, is missing. We were in Silicon Valley looking for your chips. I went into a building for a few minutes to verify that's where they were being shipped and when I came out, he was gone."

Fang sucked in some more smoke and blew it out. "And did you locate the chips?"

"I'm zeroing in on them. I should have that information soon, but I need to locate Brad first. He's a pain in the ass, I know, but he'll be a bigger pain in the ass the longer he stays missing. Did you or Jimmie happen to reclaim him?"

Fang plucked the cigarette from his lips and switched to Cantonese. The man standing next to him nodded and then said to Jack, "Mr. Fang says keeping wild monkeys would be less hassle than holding onto your brother. He doesn't have him."

"Tell him I'm sorry Brad carved up his wall but I need to find him."

The man translated. "Mr. Fang says that's your problem, not his. He wants his merchandise returned. Why are you bothering him about this?"

"Excuse me, but who are you?" Jack asked.

"I'm a golf pro. I'm giving Mr. Fang private lessons. He has a great short game. Very precise. His long irons aren't bad either. But sometimes he hooks his drive. We're working on that."

Fang pointed his cigarette as he spoke. The golf pro translated. "Mr. Fang says he can't help you. He doesn't know where your brother is. He says return to work. Find what belongs to him."

Jack spoke directly to Fang. "I visited Jimmie at his club. It's quite the operation. You should drop by. You'd be proud how the kid's turned out."

Fang hawked a rheumy globule onto the fairway. It slithered on the dewy grass. "Jimmie's not the boss yet," he said in English.

"Sometimes a father has to let the son shine," Jack said.

Fang hawked again. "It's his fault the chips were stolen. He was taken advantage of. That's very bad for business."

"But you still have your fab plant, right? Fire up the production line. Keep the chips rolling in. Flood the market before Sinclair Huntington does."

"Now you're the one who is dumb as duck." Fang switched to Cantonese.

"Mr. Fang said you are very ignorant about our culture," the golf pro translated. "Why are you wasting time looking for your brother while the chips remain in the hands of Mr. Fang's enemies?"

"Brother. In. Law. Educate me. Why is he so worried about Huntington?"

"It's not so much about the money as it is about face. Mr. Fang can't be seen as a victim. He doesn't want people to discover his son was outsmarted either. In their business, that's vital. Find the chips and save the Fangs their face."

"I plan to. But I got to save my brother-in-law's ass first. I'm going to ask straight up and straight out. If Fang didn't take Brad, does he know who did?"

Fang nodded and answered for himself. "The only logical choice is Mr. Huntington. Now you have also lost face. Get back to work."

Someone shouted from the tee box. A foursome was waiting for Fang to hit. One shook his driver and told them to hurry the fuck up. Fangs' bodyguards waved their ARs back and fired a few bursts in the air.

Fang shook his head at the scurrying foursome. "The people they're letting into the club these days. I'm going to have to speak with the membership committee."

20

Jack stood on the corner of Montgomery and Clay and stared at the tallest building in the city. When the Transamerica Pyramid was topped out in 1972, it was a middle finger to San Franciscans who worried they were becoming Manhattanized. Jack had never worked in a skyscraper beyond renting offices on a short-term basis when he needed to create a *Big Store*. Though he'd never been under the thumb of a corporate boss or forced to climb the ladder to win a corner desk, he didn't belittle or begrudge those who were. Nor did he ever con a nine-to-fiver who wasn't looking to cut corners and didn't have a streak of larceny in their heart. His sense of fair play wasn't the only reason. It also had to do with an old truism Henri LeConte taught him: you can't cheat an honest man.

There was a security desk in the Pyramid's lobby, but Jack paid it no mind as he pretend talked on his phone and strode purposefully to the elevator. He punched the button for the highest floor. The financial and operational brain trust for Sinclair Huntington's global empire occupied most of the building, but Jack didn't need a tenant directory to tell him only the highest floor with its unobstructed 360-degree view could accommodate an emperor's ego.

The doors opened to a conspicuously small, windowless reception room. There was no desk, no receptionist, and no couch or chairs. Jack pirouetted slowly, looking directly at the cameras he knew were trained on him. Infrareds were scanning his body, all but inserting a rectal thermometer. Three minutes later a door swished open and revealed a stern woman wearing a charcoal suit and candy-apple-red cheaters.

"I am afraid you do not have a scheduled appointment, sir. We do not accommodate walk-ins," she said in a crisp and very proper English accent. "The elevator will return you to the ground floor. Good day."

Jack smiled at her. "That's the same thing I told the police when they came to my front door, but they said no appointment necessary."

"I am sure I do not know what you are inferring," she said.

"I'm inferring Mr. Huntington is the reason the cops came calling. And when they show up here, they won't bother with shed-yull-ing an appointment either."

The red cheaters were slipping down her nose. She started to sputter but the door swished open again. Two men wearing charcoal suits that matched hers stood in the opening.

"If you would," one started.

"Follow us, sir," finished the other.

Neither wore red reading glasses but both spoke with English accents. They led him to a conference room with a wide-angle view of the bay. A long black conference table with matching Aeron chairs stood in the middle. Jack took a seat. The men sat across from him. They folded their hands on the table and expectantly looked at him.

"What is the nature," one said.

"Of your business?" the other finished.

"It's private," Jack said. "I'll let Huntington know when I see him."

"Mr. Huntington is quite preoccupied," the first said.

"With the tragedy that has beset his family," the second said.

"I saw the million-dollar reward," Jack started and then paused before finishing in the pair's singsong cadence. "No questions asked."

"Is that why you are here?"

The first handed off to the second. "Because of the reward?"

"Well, a million dollars is a lot of money," Jack said.

"There is a process in place for providing information," said the first.

"And any received will be treated with all sincerity," said the second.

"Time to call in the White Rabbit, Tweedledee and Tweedledum. We all know who I am and why I'm here. Huntington and I need to talk."

Before they could respond, Sinclair Huntington entered. He was wearing perfectly creased jeans, rubber-soled boating shoes without socks, and a white and gold Windbreaker. His portrait as a Jolly Roger with dollar signs as the crossed cutlasses was embroidered on the breast. Huntington's skin looked bronzed and his eyes were neither red from crying nor had shadows under them. If he was letting mourning interfere with his beauty sleep, Jack couldn't tell.

Huntington smiled thinly. "Mr. McCoul, we meet again. And as before, you come without invitation."

"I figured if I called to shed-yull an appointment, I'd be put on the equivalent of an airline standby list."

Huntington looked at his wristwatch. It was a little smaller than Big Ben and had more dials on it than a jet cockpit. "I am sure you can appreciate my time is quite limited. I will grant you a minute out of respect for my late wife. You two appeared to have some sort of personal connection, whatever it may have been."

"You might want Dee and Dum here to take a walk," Jack said

The tech titan shook his perfectly coiffed head. "On the contrary. These gentlemen are my attorneys. Given your reputation and behavior, I believe I may need their advice or at least their witness." He glanced at his watch again. "You have forty seconds remaining."

Jack took a deep breath and then exhaled. "The Fangs know you stole their chips. Your wife discovered you were bringing them in under cover of darkness to beat her out of her due in a divorce settlement. Your ruddy-faced first mate Cutler tried to bury me at Candlestick. Now he's kidnapped my brother-in-law who signed on to unload your chips. His name is Brad. You need to let him go or I call the cops. There, that took ten seconds. You owe me thirty."

Huntington arched one brow without moving the other. It was the type of pose perfected by action stars who were hired for looks, not acting ability. "Those are quite the allegations. My attorneys would be only too happy to file a lawsuit for slander and defamation of character. However, out of respect for my late wife, I will bear your ignorance and explain why you are wrong on all counts."

He gestured to the woman with the red cheaters who was standing quietly in the corner. "Ms. Tompkins, would you be so kind to push back my call with Chief Liu a few minutes? His personal update on the investigation will have to wait. Thank you."

Then he walked to a whiteboard and started drawing a series of boxes and circles connected by dots, dashes and arrows. Jack had seen taggers display more talent.

"I am afraid the Fangs have misrepresented the rightful

ownership of the microprocessors you appear fixated on," Huntington said, pointing to his diagram. "That may be because they fail to understand it themselves or given their, how shall I put it, criminal approach to business, chose to obscure the truth. It is understandable you believed them given your own criminal history. No doubt, it colors your perception of reality."

The Tweedles nodded in unison.

Huntington pointed at the whiteboard. "The Fangs did not own the silicon wafer fabrication plant where the microchips were manufactured. Unbeknownst to them, I purchased the plant. Actually, a subsidiary of mine did following the completion of a rather complex takeover of its parent company. I shall not bother to explain to you about the favorable advantages of foreign holding companies, currency exchange offsets and sovereign credit default swaps but suffice it to say, upon execution, the purchase agreement entitled me to all of the plant's tangible assets."

He circled a couple of boxes. "That included all of its facilities, equipment, contracts, and properties. The Fangs failed to secure the manufacturing of the product in question with a bona fide contract or a significant deposit, thus rendering their claim of ownership as unverifiable. Taking possession of all the plant's tangible assets, including products being manufactured or in transit that lacked legitimate provenance, was well within my legal rights. Any court of law would agree."

The attorneys imitated bobblehead dolls.

Something in Jack's stomach began to gnaw. "Would those same courts agree the Fangs still own the patents?"

"Proving patent ownership as well as infringement has always been a thorny issue in the technological industry," Huntington said.

"In other words, by the time a verdict could be made, you will have already flooded the market and moved on to the next big thing. If you wind up having to pay a penalty for violating the Fangs' patent, it will be pennies on the dollar compared to what you profited from selling them. A cost which you'll be able to write off anyway."

"Perhaps you do understand our business after all," Huntington said with a slight smile.

"And what would your courts say about passing these chips off as domestically produced? The IRS and SEC might not think kindly on that."

Huntington shook his head as if he was trying to reason with a loved one who was confined to the Alzheimer's wing. "Who is to say they are not? Any portion of a product that is manufactured here, be it a single grain of sand used to form the silicon wafer or the paper in a packing crate, makes the entire product fall within the legally accepted definition of domestically produced. I assure you my chips will meet that definition. Thus, they are entitled to the benefits the government has bestowed to incentivize local manufacturing in the name of job creation."

Jack wanted to spit. "High tech's no different than big oil. There's always a loophole you can drive a tanker through."

"A favorable position my lobbyists in Washington have worked diligently to establish, I grant you." Huntington smiled again. "And in the event of a misguided legal challenge, my attorneys will mount a vigorous defense, generating a veritable blizzard of motions, briefs and countersuits that will keep the Justice Department shoveling for years just to glimpse daylight."

"That still doesn't explain why you're smuggling them into San Francisco," Jack said.

The billionaire sighed. "Leave it to a petty criminal to see a crime where none exists. Why would I call attention to an inbound shipping container filled with a revolutionary new product? Do you have any idea how competitive my industry is? The amount of corporate spying that goes on? Secrecy is a common business strategy. The story of how Apple brought in the first iPods without their competitors getting advanced knowledge is fascinating. Sending a trial container is no different from scouting a battlefield. If your enemy is planning an ambush, it is better to risk a single scout than an entire battalion."

Jack leaned in his chair. "Nice story, but aren't you forgetting something? You didn't tell your wife about the chips. You left your own chief operating officer in the dark."

Huntington sighed again. He turned to the lawyers. "Gentlemen, how many companies have we acquired this year? How many products have we brought to market?" He turned to Jack. "Ours is a fast-paced business and our company global. Research and development is usually at least a year ahead of production. This particular acquisition will show up in our regular quarterly reporting as is required and customary. My dear late wife would have been the first to confirm this is not the first acquisition that proceeded on my approval alone. As chairman and chief executive officer I am entrusted to execute transactions as I see fit so we may take advantage of changing market conditions. If you followed the stock market, then you would know our shareholders not only approve of this, but are rewarded handsomely for their trust in me."

Huntington was as adept at spinning facts as he was unfurling sails. Still, Jack had to ask, "And my brother-in-law's disappearance? How come Cutler is so hot to find him?"

"Do you have any idea how many people I employ?" Huntington asked in an exasperated voice. "Do you think I have the time or the interest to pay attention to every little disagreement one of my workers may be having? As to your brother, Brad is it? I recall a young man by that name who ran into an unfortunate turn of luck at the Franciscan Yacht Club's annual poker tournament. If your brother lost a wager to an employee and that employee acted untoward in the collection of a debt, then I can assure you he will be disciplined appropriately."

Huntington stood. "Now I am afraid our time has run out. The chief of police is waiting to provide me with new information about the crime that took my wife's life. But before I take my leave, ask yourself this. Would a person of my stature, my wealth and my reputation steal from a gang of criminals, defraud the government and abduct a penniless gambler?" He laughed heartily as the lawyers bobbed in unison. "I must watch more television."

21

Katie wasn't there when Jack got home. He checked the gym schedule she kept fastened to the refrigerator with a miniature cable car magnet. She'd be busy for the rest of the day. There were no messages on voice mail. All he could do now was hope Brad would return on his own or at least send a message about where he was hiding out. That was, if he were able.

Jack stared out the window at the freighters in line at the Port of Oakland. He had no choice but to keep searching for the chips no matter what Sinclair Huntington told him. Besides, the tech mogul's explanations about how he'd outmaneuvered the Fangs and why he hadn't told Mai about the chips were too glib. Jack could sense Huntington's feeling of entitlement, that winning was his right not a reward. The odds of bringing him down were a hundred-to-one long shot, but Jack wasn't afraid to try. It was the same as when he used to play baseball. He always had his best game when the other team was stacked with ringers.

Jack used the fab plant's address in Santa Clara to search public records. It didn't take long to find a copy of a recently filed fictitious business name. The property was registered to a business named Triangulum. Sinclair Huntington's name was nowhere in sight and the layers of holding companies and attorney firms were like Russian nesting dolls. Each time Jack pulled one off, another lay beneath. The deeper he dug, the more he realized somebody was hiding something.

Googling Triangulum took him to a Wikipedia entry. Triangulum was the most distant galaxy visible to the naked eye, but what caught his eye was a reference to Chinese astronomy under History and Mythology. The stars of Triangulum were part of the Great Celestial General, the fifth paranatellon of the second house of the White Tiger of the West. Huntington named the company after a mythological god as big as his own ego.

The online drayage directory listed seventy trucking outfits. Jack could've started with the *a*'s and worked his way down, but he rolled the dice instead and started dialing. After crapping out six times, seven came up lucky.

"Eagle Express," the receptionist answered. "We really shake our tail for you."

Jack deepened his voice. "Yeah, Jerry Landers at Triangulum, here. Boss wants me to double-check our pickup and delivery."

"I'll connect you to scheduling and dispatch."

Jack tapped on the link to San Francisco Bay's AIS live tracker while he waited. Little blinking arrows indicating the name and location of ships streamed across the screen.

Another voice came on, another woman. She asked what he needed. He gave her the same line. "I'll need the order number," she said officiously.

"That's just it," Jack said. "We're still moving in and the computer system has more glitches than a Florida election. Can you look it up on your end if I give you the name and address? I'd really appreciate it." He spelled Triangulum and provided the street name and number. When she gave a tired sigh, he said, "Please? It'll get the boss off my back. I'm new here and I really need this job. Three kids. Two in braces and one needs new soccer shoes. The bills, they never end."

The woman sighed. "Don't I know it. All right, give me a minute." Her fingernails made a clicking sound as she typed. "Here it is. Triangulum. We have you scheduled."

Jack decided to keep with Katie's strategy of working back to front. "Thanks. How about the ETA? Like I said, it's a madhouse here and I got to be sure I got enough hands on deck to unload a TEU."

"We only give four hour windows," the woman said. "Traffic being what it is and any delays at the port that are beyond our control."

"No worries. Four hours is fine."

"Let me see. Going to Santa Clara, that would make it in the afternoon, between one and five."

"Okay, I'll alert receiving for tomorrow."

"What? Wait. Not tomorrow. The day after."

"You should see the boss's handwriting. It's like a doctor's." Jack checked the AIS. Four ships matched the docking time. "I can't make out the ship's name. It looks like *Jiangxi*."

"Not even close."

"This is ridiculous. The *Integrity*?"

"You're kidding. His *s*'s look like *i*'s?"

"Oh, I got it now. The *Sincerity*. Berth 23."

"I hope you guys get your computers up and running," she said. "You need them."

"You're telling me. Hey, wait a sec, the boss didn't list the serial shipping container code. Do you have it?"

"That's odd. I'm reading the electronic record and it says the number is TK." The dispatcher paused. "To come. But don't worry. There must have been a misprint on the shipper's end.

I'm sure someone's checking on it and the code will be inputted correctly by the time the ship docks."

Huntington was hiding the container's ID until the last possible moment, but Jack couldn't wait that long. He needed the number and he needed now.

22

It was another typical San Francisco morning, which meant the fog hung so close to the choppy water that Jack hoped the captain wouldn't crash into Alcatraz as they ploughed across the bay toward Sausalito. He had the outbound ferry to himself. All the commuters were heading in the opposite direction, and it was still too early in the morning for tourists. Jack usually stood on the deck for the thirty-minute crossing but instead he was slouched in a seat, cradling a paper cup of coffee and listening to a podcast. Sinclair Huntington was telling a *Marketplace* reporter he was going to attend the gamer convention despite his wife's murder. The product he'd be debuting was sure to change the world, he said, and Mai would want him to be there.

"He makes P.T. Barnum sound like a vacuum salesman," Jack said, unaware he was speaking out loud because of the earbuds.

The engine slowed and the horn blared as the ferry entered Sausalito's postcard harbor. Jack crossed the gangplank and walked up Gate Five Road to a motley flotilla of houseboats. A brown shingle cottage built atop an old gravel barge was moored at the end of the furthest dock. It had blue trimmed windows and matching flower boxes filled with geraniums. An ancient white standard poodle snoozed on a redwood deck. Jack extracted half a bagel from his coat pocket and Frisbeed it over the low white picket fence. The pooch snagged it without opening his eyes.

"Attaboy, Chagall. Henri home?"

The dog woofed hoarsely and the front door opened. "Don't spoil him," Henri LeConte said. "He only eats brie and foie gras as it is."

"And whose fault is that? You let him sit at the table."

"Love me, love my dog."

"For a guy born in Daly City you're more Parisian than the Eifel Tower."

The debonair con artist smiled. "I suppose you want coffee."

"That and some advice, if you're feeling up to it."

"*Mon dieu,* I've never been down in my life." Beneath his blue beret, Henri winked, turned his aluminum walker around, and shuffled into the houseboat.

The main living area was adorned with framed watercolors he had painted—mostly seascapes. They were good. Henri always had a keen eye and steady hands, skills that had served him well as an art forger and documents counterfeiter when he was running international arts and antiquities scams.

Jack took a seat at the galley table. It was covered with copies of the *Daily Racing Form*. "I didn't know you could still get this in print."

Henri pushed the plunger on a french press and then filled two mugs. "I prefer the feel of paper in my hand, to hear it crinkle, smell the ink, doodle in the margins. Besides, if I fall asleep reading a computer, it might fall and smack me in my *pierre*." He slid the mug over. "It still works, in case you were wondering."

"I wasn't." Jack sipped the coffee. It was strong.

Jack was fond of the old grifter and his old world charm.

Henri had taken him under his wing when Jack was first starting out, teaching him how to spot a mark, stage a play, and walk off with the award as the final curtain fell. Best of all, Henri taught him never to con himself into believing he couldn't get caught. Before his stroke, Henri was light on his feet, quick of wit, a *bon vivant* in the classic sense. He ate lunch every day at Le Central and never missed the black-tie galas for the ballet, symphony, and opera. "Cultivating clients," he'd always say with a wink, his pencil moustache twitching.

"How's the painting going?" Jack asked.

"Ah, you can see for yourself I am in a creative rut." Henri waved his mug at the wall of small masterpieces. "I need a change of scenery, a change of subject matter. Nudes, that is what I am thinking. A switch in medium too. Oils on large canvases. Life-size."

"You got a new physical therapist coming in, that it? What happened to Nurse Ratchett?"

"She went to work at the burn unit at Marin General. She professed to miss hopping on her patients and peeling away the dead skin. Debriding while riding, she called it." Henri shuddered.

"And the new PT?"

Henri smiled. "Milinka. She is a beauty beyond any the masters painted. None of them, not Matisse, Giacometti, even Picasso, had a model like her. Milinka is a Serbian refugee. Her skin is as soft as oysters. Her name means grace and she overflows with it." He looked off dreamily.

"Careful you don't blow another gasket, Henri. You're running out of valves they can replace."

"My goal in life is to die in the same manner as Félix François Faure."

Jack grinned. He'd heard Henri often repeat the scandalous story of how the former French president had died *in flagrante* with his mistress. He recited the punch line: " 'Your last thoughts were thinking you were coming when you were actually going.' "

Henri's chuckle turned into a cough. He put a napkin to his lips. "Speaking of beautiful women, how is the lovely Katie? The sweetest move you ever pulled was convincing her to say *oui*."

Jack tipped his mug at him. Henri returned the gesture with a gentlemanly bow. "Of course, a close second is that move you pulled on the Moogasian Gallery job. I must say, you made your dear professor proud."

Jack hadn't been in the game for very long. At least not at the level Henri played. The old forger was working on selling a notorious private art collector a Richard Diebenkorn. The hook was Henri let the mark know it was all part of a scam. Henri showed him the forgery he'd made. The original hung in one of the city's foremost art galleries. Henri knew the collector had a long-running feud with the gallery's owner. He convinced the mark he would swap the fake for the original and sell it to him. The collector bit, blinded to the possibility of a double switch and by the thought of getting the real painting while pulling a fast one on his rival.

Henri painted two forgeries and swapped one for the original and handed the other over to the mark. To convince him it was the original, Henri had to prove the forgery he sneaked into Moogasian's was indeed a fake. Jack devised the solution himself. He took on the role of a tourist visiting the gallery and stumbled with a grande latte in his hand. The drink splashed the forgery. The paint ran, exposing a pentimento underneath. Bobby Ballena, playing another tourist, videoed the scene with his phone for proof. The mark never doubted he received the original, which Henri had already sold to a private collector in Berlin.

"Just followed your KISS advice," Jack said. "The smarter the mark, the simpler the play. Big men don't look for anything small."

The door pushed open and Chagall nosed his way in. The poodle was half-blind but knew every inch of the houseboat by smell and went immediately to his master and laid his soft muzzle on Henri's knee.

"I would be dishonest if I said I did not miss the life," Henri said, his eyes downcast as he scratched the dog's ears. "I followed my own advice and got out when I could not play 100 percent anymore. It is a lot better off than old athletes who hang on too long. Still, it leaves a hole. Everything about who you are, what you did, it's all behind you now. Sometimes you wake up and have to check your passport to remember your own name. You try to tell yourself you still have it, you could still do it, but then you remember the easiest person to con is yourself."

Henri scratched the dogs ears some more. "Would you listen to me go on. I sound like some Gitanes-smoking existentialist. *Do be do be do.*" He laughed, holding his silk handkerchief to his lips.

Jack knew that could be him someday if he didn't stay out of the game. Every player had an exit plan, all right, but few ever took it. There was always one more play to make, the big score right around the corner. But Jack told himself he was different. He met Katie and had pulled the ripcord long before he hit the ground.

Henri smiled. "But you are not here to listen to an old man reminisce. What do you want to know that you do not know already?"

Jack took a breath and then laid it all out as simply as he could. Henri didn't nod or take notes, the gentlemanly grifter relying on his photographic memory, which had allowed him to mimic masterpieces. After Jack finished, Henri sat expressionless. Minutes passed before he spoke.

"Let us put the murder aside for a moment and focus on Katie's brother. He's your connection to the chips. Could lightning really have struck twice?"

"If anybody could get himself snatched again it's Brad," Jack said. "He's always been unlucky."

"But you say the Fangs didn't reclaim him."

"They had no reason. I was already looking for their chips."

"So if not them, then who?"

"The obvious choice would be Sinclair Huntington. He has the most to gain by keeping Brad quiet," Jack said.

"And also the most to lose. From what you have told me, Huntington has developed plausible explanations for all that you accuse him. It would be his word against Brad's. We both know who the authorities would find the more credible." Henri shook his head. "No, if Huntington is responsible for his wife's murder, then he would not risk calling attention to himself with a needless abduction. It must be someone else."

"The wild card," Jack said.

Henri looked pleased. "You remember what I taught you. No game is without one. Who is it?"

Jack steeled himself. "Caspar Brixton."

The mere mention of his name caused Henri's mood to darken immediately. "That piece of *merde* is out of prison? You are working with him again? I cannot believe it. I warned you about him the last time. Did you not learn your lesson?"

Jack drank his coffee. It had grown cold. Five years ago he had gone against Henri's advice when Brix had asked for help. Henri told Jack Brix couldn't be trusted. He knew from experience.

Brix had grown up in Sausalito. His father was a small-time drug dealer. The Brixtons lived aboard an old scow that was tied up a few docks over from where Henri's tidy houseboat was moored. As a boy, Brix earned a reputation for cruelty and recklessness. He hid fishhooks inside anchovies and fed them to the pelicans. He robbed neighboring houseboats and then would steal a sailboat to make his getaway. He ran more than one neighbor's boat aground on Angel Island. One night the Brixtons' scow caught fire and burned to the waterline. Brix's father went down with the ship. Literally. Most people thought he had fallen asleep smoking marijuana, but there were others who pointed to the bad blood between father and son. The police were never able to prove anything, but Henri had little doubt of the boy's guilt. When the old forger found out his protégé Jack was thinking of working with Brix, he tried everything he could to convince him otherwise. But Jack, who was feeling the need to separate from another father figure, wouldn't listen. It turned out to be huge mistake.

Jack pushed away the coffee mug. "Brix found me." He proceeded to tell Henri how Brix had accosted him at the Farmer's Market and again outside of Jimmie Fang's club.

Henri grew thoughtful again. "He may have picked up Brad to get information. He knows you would never give it to him. The first question is what will Brix do to Brad once he gets it? The second is what will Brix do that could jeopardize you finding the chips? He stands between you and identifying Mrs. Huntington's killer."

"You've always had a way of seeing the whole board," Jack said. "All that chess you play. What else am I missing here?"

"The obvious question. Could Brix also be the killer?"

"I don't see how. He showed up pretty late in the game. It was after the Fangs enlisted me to find the chips. I've never told Brix about them. Even if he has been following me, he wouldn't have been able to put two and two together until I parked out front of the chip plant."

Henri raised an eyebrow. "And no one else might have told him?"

"Who? Huntington? The Fangs? Why would they?"

Henri fixed his gaze on Jack. "So remind me, when did Brix first approach you?"

"At the Farmer's Market."

"After you met with the Fangs. After you started searching for the chips."

"That's right."

Henri's knowing look didn't waver; it was not lost on Jack. He wanted to smack himself. "And later that night Mai was murdered," he said in a tone of resignation.

Henri smiled. "What is that clever little saying you have? Something about coincidences?"

Jack pushed away from the table. "Thanks for the coffee and the advice. I got to go find those chips."

"There is one more thing," Henri said.

"Yeah, what's that?" Jack said impatiently.

"Your plan for taking the chips once you locate them. I imagine they will command a considerable sum."

"They're only worth as much as my freedom and Brad's life. I'm trading information, not stealing. No way I'm going to risk that."

The old forger stood and held onto his walker. His eyes twinkled. "Ah, my young friend. You may not have a choice."

23

Every time Meaghan's number appeared on caller ID Jack wanted a stiff drink. He wondered if his sister was some kind of cosmic payback, a spiritual slap from Heaven to atone for his misdeeds or an early preview of what he could expect in hell. Either way, he had no choice but to continue looking out for her.

"What do you need now?" was how he answered. "I already gave your landlord the back rent, paid the utilities, and threatened Derrick with jail or the hospital if he ever smacked you around again."

"I called to say thanks," Meaghan said, her voice sounding sweet and excited. "And you don't have to worry about me and the kids anymore."

Jack had heard it before. It usually lasted for as long as it took Derrick to drink her grocery money.

"Glad to hear it." He was on his way to the Mission to meet with Hark. "Derrick really get himself into a program? You clean the house?"

"What? No. I mean, yes, the house is clean, well pretty clean, but Derrick? No, I'm going to do what you said. We're through. I'm making it official. I'm calling that lawyer."

Jack pulled the Prius to the curb. He was on Harrison Street just under the Central Freeway. A homeless man, slumped next to a wobbly shopping cart stuffed with green trash bags, stared at Jack hopefully, his bleary eyes black beads swimming in deep pools of wino red. Even though the window was shut, his wet dog stink rolled in.

"You're kidding, right?" Jack said.

Meaghan sighed. "Why do you say that? Don't you know how hard it's been on me? I try. Every damn day I try."

The homeless man was leaning on his cart, pawing through the bags. He brought out a greasy cardboard sign. It was upside down, but Jack could still read it. Down on My Luck So Give a Fuck and Fork Over a Buck. Jack decided he'd throw the guy a twenty to mark the occasion.

"Well, good for you, M.," Jack said. "It's what you should do."

"Don't you want to know why the change of heart?" she said, her voice turning girlish.

"Sure I do."

She giggled. "I met someone."

"What do you mean *met*? Who?"

"I followed your advice. You said I should find a man who would treat me right and I did."

Jack exhaled loudly into the phone. "That was quick. What kind of guy?"

"A nice guy. Real nice."

"Where did you meet him?"

"That's the thing. It was kismet. That's what he called it. Kismet. You know what it means?"

"I got a pretty good idea. Where did you meet him, a bar?"

"Be nice. Here at home. He knocked on the door. He's a

survey taker, like the census, only more types of questions. He's really nice and has a good job. You'd like him."

Jack's radar ratcheted up. A guy with a clipboard and a stick-on name tag most likely was casing the place. "What kind of questions did he ask you?"

"What you'd expect. Name, age, not that I told him. A girl's got to have her secrets. How long I lived here, how many kids, that sort of thing."

"And what did he say when you told him you were married?"

Meaghan hesitated. "Well, when he asked my status, I told him it was complicated. Like what you put on Facebook. And that's when I found out what a really nice guy he is. We speak the same language. He tells me how his marriage fell apart. How his wife, well, he didn't say it like this, but I could tell she was a real bitch. And we were standing there talking and then I said, why don't you come in; I'll make you a cup of coffee and we can finish the interview sitting down." She took a deep breath. "Jesus, Mary and Joseph, he's real nice. You'd like him."

"Were the kids home? He try anything?"

"Jesus, Jackie. I told you he's nice. And, no, the kids weren't home. You think I'd let a stranger inside, even a nice one like him?"

"So, are you going to see him again?"

"I already did. After we finished talking, he said he had to get to work. That's the kind of guy he is. Dedicated to his job. A real hard worker. You can tell. But he asked me out. In a nice way. And I said, sure, why not? And so we went out last night. He took me to this really fancy place. It was French. Or it could've been Italian. Anyway, it was so good. Expensive too."

Jack, his radar notching up even higher, said, "He can afford that on a survey taker's salary?"

"God, you're so suspicious. Sometimes I don't know why I bother talking to you. I thought you'd be happy for me."

"Hey, you're my sister. And I am happy for you. So what's Mr. Nice Guy's name?"

Meaghan laughed. "You won't believe it. Remember that old cartoon we used to watch as kids? The one with the friendly ghost?"

Jack's knuckles turned white as they gripped the steering wheel.

HARK MET him at Mel's Drive-in on Lombard Street. Jack was sitting in a tan and green vinyl booth with a plate of untouched french fries and a Diet Coke. The wrapper was still on the top half of the straw.

"You going eat those?" Hark asked, sliding in across from him.

"Knock yourself out. I ordered them to hold the table."

Hark grinned. "Go ahead, have one. I won't tell Katie."

"Brix is in a motel down the street," Jack said. "He wanted me to know he's there. It's why he told Meaghan where he's staying."

Hark took the bottle of catsup, unscrewed the cap, and slapped his palm on the bottom. A red plop landed beside the heap of golden fries. He picked one up, dunked it, and with a pinky in the air, chewed it slowly, savoring it as if it were a tender stalk of asparagus dipped in béarnaise sauce.

"I got to say, *vato*. Growing up? I had a thing for your sister. All due respect. She was mighty fine. If it weren't for you... Well, I didn't, but I woulda. It's a compliment; you hear what I'm saying?"

Jack started drumming the table. "Brix blames me for that lame-ass play of his. Now I wish they'd given him a ten spot."

Hark licked the catsup off his fingers. "When I was 'banging, a guy do something like this, crossing the line and threatening another 'banger's family, he got taken out. Period. End of story."

"I already told him if I see him around my loft, see him around Katie, I'd have him picked up for breaking parole." Jack's face grew tight. "Or worse."

Hark beamed and slapped the table with his french fry–free hand. "That's what I'm talking about. Glad to hear you strapped on a pair. Not that I had my doubts you would, especially she being your sister and Katie being Katie."

Jack kept drumming his fingers. "Brix is adding complications I don't need. I visited Henri LeConte. He got me thinking that it was Brix that did Huntington's wife."

"Really?"

"I'm not completely convinced about that, but if he took Brad, for sure he knows about the chips. I can't have him blowing everything up." Jack pulled out some bills. Too many to cover fries and a Diet Coke. "Time to talk to our not so friendly ghost."

Hark frowned at the plate. "You think I got time to get these put in a doggie bag?"

THEY LEFT their cars in Mel's parking lot and walked to the motel. It was old-fashioned, the kind found along highways the interstate bypassed. There were two floors of rooms wrapped around a scuffed parking lot.

Jack held up his hand when they reached the driveway. "Brix's got a room upstairs. I'll go talk to him. You wait here."

"If the dude's a turkey like you say, better I come with you. I can hold him down in the tub while you talk some sense into him," Hark said. "Dudes in tubs listen better. They'll tell you anything you ask. They know they're in there 'cause it makes washing the blood down the drain easier."

"You learn that clearing houses in Afghanistan?"

Hark shook his head. "Tubs are Mission-style all the way."

"Brix will be expecting me but I can handle him all right. It's who he's got coming in behind me you need to stop. Brix's the sort who stacks the deck. He'll think I'll keep my eyes on him and not the jokers he's hiding."

"I shoulda thought of that on my own. I'm getting soft being a legit businessman. Okay *'mano,* I got your back." Hark opened the doggy bag, dumped out the fries, and stuck the Beretta M9 in it. He held it at the ready.

Brix was staying in a middle unit. Jack rapped on the door and stepped to the side.

"That you, Jack?" Brix called.

"Can't get anything past you," Jack said.

The door swung open. Brix was dressed in khaki Dickies and a black V-neck T-shirt. The short sleeves showed off a swastika and other Aryan Brotherhood prison tats. "Meaghan's sure a sweet piece of ass," he said.

Jack saw it for the red cape it was and ignored it. "Your friends won't be joining us. Just letting you know."

"All my friends are still in the joint. Except for you. We're still friends, aren't we, Jack? Maybe even soon to be brothers-in-law." Brix grinned.

Jack rolled his shoulders. "Where's Brad?"

"Who's Brad?"

"My brother-in-law. What did I tell you about leaving my family alone?"

"Hey, I'm out of prison now. I don't need fish. Especially now that I got Meaghan." He leered.

"I'm not going to say it again. You need to let Brad go, stay away from my sister, and back the fuck off."

Brix went to a beat-up dresser that held a clunky TV, bottle of Wild Turkey, and two plastic bathroom cups. He poured whiskey in both cups and held one out. Jack didn't take it. He wanted to keep both hands free.

"What do I need your brother for?" Brix said. "I've known about the chips from the start. Jimmie Fang told me. How this computer geek ripped them off. How the geek's bringing them in on a ship in a big metal box. How the Fangs grabbed your brother and are making you look for the chips. How if you don't find them, Jimmie's going to turn your brother into fish food and you with him. How the computer geek's wife got her neck broke. How the cops think you did it."

Brix took a breath, drank some of the Wild Turkey. "Careful, McCoul. Your mouth's hanging open. You're wondering why Jimmie told me all that shit. Don't you get it? I'm the insurance policy. The Fangs wanted backup in case you weren't up to the job. And after following you around? I'd say you're not." He downed the rest of his drink. "You get it yet? I'm not only in this thing, I'm running the show now. You're just the stuffed bunny sent out of the box for the greyhounds to chase. Or should I say, your pal the cop."

Jack held his hands to his side but clenched his fists. "We'll see about who's running what."

Brix finished the other plastic cup full of bourbon in a single gulp and grinned again. "The only thing you've been right about so far is my friends. Only they're not out in the parking lot waiting to come and shoot you in the head. They're sitting in a car parked outside of your sister's. I don't call them in five minutes, call them regular like, they go inside." He let it hang. "So get the fuck out of here, and find the chips."

24

That night Jack and Katie went to dinner in North Beach. Bella Luna occupied a tiny storefront on Green Street and was wedged between a Laundromat and a corner grocery with Parma hams and salamis hanging behind the counter. The restaurant was sized right and paced slow. It only had eight tables and diners never felt rushed by the staff. That wasn't the only reason Bella Luna was among Jack and Katie's favorites. It also served the best tagliolini alla frantoiana this side of Siena, and its wine list included a succulent Brunello di Montalcino.

They had a window table. Katie was people watching. Jack studied the label on the wine bottle—it was decorated with hummingbirds—as he went over in his mind what he was about to tell her. He sipped some wine. There was no way to sugarcoat bad news so he took a gulp.

"Easy there, cowboy," Katie said with a laugh. "Since when did we chug our special Brunello like it was a beer?" Jack put the glass down and wiped his mouth. His hesitation triggered her intuition. "What is it?" she asked. "What's wrong?"

"It's Brad. He's missing."

Katie's favorite earrings always brought out the sparkle in her green eyes, but now they clouded with worry. "What do you mean?"

Jack took her hand. "I've looked for him everywhere. I don't know where he is. I'm sorry, babe. I didn't mean for this to happen. Any of it."

"But you told me when you came home from Silicon Valley you dropped him off at his apartment. You lied to me."

"Only because I didn't want you to worry. I thought I could find him."

"It's because of the chips, isn't it?" Her tone was accusatory. "Did those men in Chinatown kidnap him again?"

Jack glanced around the room. The other diners didn't appear to have heard her. "No," he said softly. "There's a chance Brad's simply hiding. He's pretty scared."

Katie raised her chin. "He would've called me and told me where he's at. Brad doesn't like me to worry."

Jack kept his opinion to himself. "I'm doing everything I can to find him."

"Well, you're not doing a very good job." She pulled her hand away.

"Babe," he said. "I'm trying hard here, but Brad brought this on himself."

"I'm going to call Terry," she said. "We need the police's help. Brad could be in danger. Maybe the same person who killed that woman took him. Oh my god."

There was no way Jack was going to tell Katie about Meaghan or Brix. He crossed his arms. "We can't call the cops. If someone did take Brad, and I'm not sure that they did, then the only way to save him is with the chips. I got a plan. You got to trust me."

Katie closed her eyes and took a deep breath, held it, and

then blew it out slowly. Jack recognized the yoga technique. She called it centering herself. "Tell it to me," she said.

"No. You can't be involved in this."

She threw her napkin on the table. "I'm already involved. Brad's my brother. You're my husband." This time people did stare.

Jack picked up his glass of wine and swished it. "It could be that I need to do more than find the chips," he said in a low voice. "Do you understand what I'm saying? If I tell you anything more, that would make you an accessory. I won't do that. You got to trust me."

She tightened her lips. "I'm your wife. I do trust you. But you have to trust me too. Didn't I help you figure out a way to locate where the chips were going? I'm already an accessory."

"This is different," he said. "There's no crime in finding the chips. But there sure as hell is if I rip them off."

He polished off his glass of Brunello and sat back in his chair, daring her to try to talk him out of it.

"Okay, I understand," she said a little too quickly. "Now let's order dinner. I'm famished."

25

In the morning Katie went off to teach a yoga class and Jack sat at his dining table shuffling a deck of cards and running through a repertoire of riffles, slides, Corgis, and Hindus. Cards helped him concentrate. His mother had taught him how to play. On the nights his father spent at the firehouse, she'd round up the kids to play Clue and Monopoly. It was a way to keep them inside and out of trouble. Jack's brothers were soon ducking out to play electronic games and Meaghan retreated to her bedroom. Down to the two of them, Jack's mom turned to cards and taught him gin. When the cancer spread and she was too weak to hold a hand, he'd deal her solitaire and make the moves for her. When she started drifting in and out of consciousness, he'd sit on the edge of her bed and practice tricks. He started with palming and snap changes and then moved on to sleights and vanishes.

Jack took his game on the road after she died. He rode the muni, dealing three-card monte on top of a cardboard box in the back of the bus and hustling adults who thought they could beat a kid out of twenty dollars. The marks never stood a chance. Jack's quick hands guaranteed it. He would accidentally on purpose crease the queen of hearts so the mark would follow it not knowing that Jack had straightened it and creased a black king on the very next shuffle. And if the mark was able to pick the red lady, shills like Hark and Bobby Ballena were there to yank the bell cord. As the bus slowed for a stop Jack would scoop up the cash and crash out the emergency door and hit the asphalt running.

Jack eventually graduated from cards to computers and more elaborate cons like the ones he pulled with Henri Le Conte. But three-card monte remained at the heart of every game. No matter how elaborate the play, the key ingredients were always the same. The bait was an easy payoff and the mark was led to believe he could beat the system.

Jack cut the three face cards from the deck and started sliding them across the table. He pictured Brix as the king of spades, Sinclair Huntington the king of clubs, and the container of microchips the queen of hearts. Just like monte, he had to keep his eye on the queen if he was going to win. The Fangs may have hired Brix as backup, but he was going to double-cross them. Jack was sure of it. The chips were too valuable. Whoever controlled the chips, controlled the game. Jack could use them to outfox Brix, protect Meaghan and Brad, and, hopefully, flush out Mai's killer.

No matter what Brix thought, Jack still had the edge. He knew the name of the ship and he had found a way to identify the serial shipping container code so he could find the chips among the thousands of TEUs on board. But he still needed a way to play it all. He kept sliding the cards facedown on the table, switching the position of the queen and black kings as he stared across the bay at the lineup of cargo ships. And then he had it. The one person who could help him control the con was as regular as clockwork. Jack checked his watch and then hurried for the gym.

~

"Leo the software lion," Jack said as he stepped out of the elevator and spotted the young shipping app genius.

"Oh, hello, Jack. You startled me. Any word about the Series A funding? Time's running out on divesting my stock options. I really need to know where I'm going to put the gains."

"We need to talk."

Jack led Leonard to the massage room on the other side of the lockers. It smelled like eucalyptus, spearmint, and Bengay. He hopped on the light brown calf skin table and made a face as if he were gearing up to tell a friend not only was his wife screwing the mailman, but she'd left the door open and his dog got out and was struck by a car.

"I have to warn you," Jack said. "I'm going to use a word that makes my tongue blister. They want you to be patient."

Leonard struggled to mask his disappointment. "For how long?"

"Long enough. I don't like it any better than you do but that's the world we live in. Bankers. Underwriters. Risk managers." Jack let Leonard dangle for a while before reeling him back in. "But there is a silver lining."

"What do you mean?"

"When I told Big Angel about you, he said, smart kid." Jack nodded a couple of times. "Yep. Smart kid."

"What did he mean by that?"

"Means he knows who you are. Big Angel knows all, sees all. He has a big interest in your enterprise."

Leonard puffed out his scawny chest. "Well, my app is a very beneficial tool. We're continually updating it and adding new features all the time. Push notifications, new levels of security, enhanced monitoring and a built-in tracker should a container be lost or hijacked."

"If Big Angel likes what he sees, then Big Angel gets what he likes."

"But we're a public company now. We may not be the biggest enterprise, but we're growing." Leonard crossed his arms. "We're not for sale."

"Everything's for sale for the right price."

"Not my company."

"Admirable," Jack said. "And that's what I told Big Angel you'd say. But if Big Angel wanted to launch a hostile takeover, he'd have done it already. He wouldn't have cared how big the golden parachutes were, how nasty the poison pills. He would've bought all the public shares using the Tokyo and Hong Kong stock exchanges while you were asleep. You would've woken up in the morning to find your desk already dumped on the sidewalk. No, Big Angel wants to be a real angel here. He wants to take you to the next level."

Leonard cocked his head and squinted. "How so?"

"He wants to make a big investment. No strings attached. Omaha-style."

"How big?"

"How big do you need? What will it take to lock up the entire market, to make sure every TEU in the world is wearing your 3-D QR transponder? To secure every patent so some hacker living in his momma's basement in the Ukraine can't open source your ass?"

"He can do that?"

Jack rested his foot on his knee. "This is a twofer opportunity. You give Big Angel the word you're interested and he'll resolve this patience issue and open the door to the Series A."

"Why, that's perfect. How soon can I meet him?"

"Right away. Well, after the test, that is."

"What test?"

"You know Big Angel's reputation. He didn't study a P&L

statement or talk to industry analysts before he invested a billion in GM. He went to the nearest Buick dealer and took a Regal out for a test drive. Said it told him everything he needed to know."

"So he wants to—"

"Take your 3-D QR for a spin."

"That's even better," Leonard said. "We have a brand new multimedia sales presentation. It's killer. Industrial Light & Magic did the animation. They say George Lucas oversaw the final editing himself. It won an Eddy."

Jack held up his hand. "Big Angel's got ADHD. He'd never sit through it. Absolutely, positively hates sales pitches. No, he wants to conduct his own test. He wants you to provide him with an off-the-shelf 3-D QR transponder and the instructions that go with it. He's going to slap it on a shipping container and track it himself. He also needs to be able to track a second container that's already in transit with one of your devices on it as a control."

"Well, there's no problem giving him our newest model."

"And access to a TEU with a tracking transponder already on it?"

"Does he have to have that?"

Jack nodded. "You're an engineer. Every lab test needs a control to establish a baseline. Personally, I think the old guy just wants to race the two. But, hey, if he gets his kicks playing Mario Kart with a couple of shipping containers, who are we to judge?"

Leonard shook his head vehemently. "I can't. It would be a violation of our confidentiality agreement with customers. We would never reveal a container's code to an unauthorized third party."

"But Big Angel is only going to track it, not hijack it."

"Our reputation is based on our ability to provide customers with guaranteed security. We lose that, we're finished."

"Big Angel wouldn't tell anyone."

"I can't do it." Leonard folded his arms across his chest tighter. "I won't do it."

"Understood. I'll let Big Angel know." Jack slid off the massage table. "Admirable. Truly admirable."

"Wait. He'd only be tracking it for control purposes, right?"

"Sure, what else would he want it for?"

"Well, I suppose we could make an exception this one time as long as we kept it, uh, confidential."

"It won't leave the vault."

Leonard scrunched his baby face." You promise?"

"Cross my heart."

"Okay. I'll make sure he gets everything he needs."

"I'll make it easier," Jack said. "Give it to me and I'll walk him through it."

"Perfect. Does he already have a cargo ship and port of entry in mind?"

Jack faced the door so Leonard couldn't see his grin. "I believe he does."

JACK WALKED across the gym to the yoga studio. Despite what Katie said last night, he wanted to hear her assurances again that she wouldn't get involved any deeper. The lights were low inside the glass-fronted room, and Jack could make out the shadowy figures of several women transitioning from the Happy Baby pose to the full kundalini Lotus position. Sitar music was snaking beneath the closed door. Usually Katie assumed the one-legged Bird of Paradise as she called out different positions to her students but even in the darkness, Jack could tell something wasn't right. The silhouette at the front of the class was too tall, too heavy. His stomach churned. Red lights flashed. Jack threw open the door and charged in, bouncing across the rubber floor, hurdling a couple of yoginis.

"The schedule says Katie is supposed to be leading this class. Where is she?" he demanded.

"Please," the instructor hissed. "We're flowing from *prana* to *sushumna*. You're disrupting our aura. You'll have to leave."

Jack grabbed her arm. "I'm not going anywhere until you tell me where Katie is."

The instructor tried to maintain the Mountain Pose, her hands steepled beneath her chin. "You need to calm yourself. Find your center. I'll talk to you after we reach *sahasrara*."

"Hey, I don't have time for any fucking *namaste*. Where's Katie?"

The instructor plopped onto both feet and exhaled in frustration. "Katie asked me to substitute. She told me if I saw you to tell you she'd spoken to your sister and was going to go see her boyfriend. Your sister's boyfriend. Something about him and Katie's brother. I don't know what. It was all very confusing. Anyway, she said to say she figured out a way to help and you'd understand."

In the gloom, Jack saw Brix's feral eyes shining. Katie unwittingly walked into his lair. Jack realized he wasn't the only one playing monte as the face cards morphed into Brad and Meaghan and Katie. The sinuous sound of a sitar grew louder as Jack felt guilt wrapping around him and squeezing the air from his lungs. There wasn't a yoga move in the world that would allow him to transcend this kind of remorse, and he dropped to his knees.

Jack couldn't con himself any longer. He'd blown it big time. He'd missed the obvious—of course the Fangs would double down to save face. He missed that Brix had been playing him from the start. Missed when Brix said Mai's neck had been snapped. How could he know that? The cops never reported it. Worst of all, he missed that Katie had been serious about wanting—no, needing—to help. He let her walk straight into danger.

The yoginis in the darkened room were staring at him, but all Jack could see was Katie. Hark had been right when he said Katie brought out a different side in Jack. When they moved in together, he laughed at all the stuff she brought with her. Besides the little stone Buddha he'd coldcocked Terry Dolan with, there was a poster showing the signs of the zodiac and their corresponding Kama Sutra positions. There were dozens of cookbooks with recipes for foods he'd never heard of. But Jack soon came to appreciate Katie's astrology and everything that went with it.

Jack also brought out a different side in Katie. When they were spooning in the sack, Katie would tell him that he was the yin and she the yang. He was the dark one, and not just because of being Black Irish; it was the way he approached life. He knew what went down in the shadows. He knew people could be evil. She was the opposite. Katie was self-aware enough to know she was a force of positive human nature. "But a couple is like the tide," she said. "It takes water coming in and water going out to make it work. When we're together it's as beautiful as San Francisco Bay."

Jack realized what Katie was doing. She was purposely pushing Brix in order to reverse the direction of the flow of events and return their control to Jack. He also realized something else. The best thing about yoga room rubber floors was they made bouncing back all the easier.

26

Speeding to St. Joseph's, Jack punched it through three yellow lights and ran a red. He double-parked and took the stairs two at a time. The heavy front door was unlocked. The air inside the thick-walled church was cool and reeked of incense. Soft candlelight and the coo of doves nesting in the eaves did little to calm him down. As he hurried toward the altar, he checked the pews. A solitary figure sat in the front row but it was not who Jack expected.

"Come, my son, and sit," Father Bernardus said in a voice thin with age but still commanding. "I know why you are here. Let us wait for Inspector Dolan together."

"Jesus," Jack said in surprise.

"Still blaspheming, I see," the old priest said. "Yours has always been a rocky path. Come, sit. Terry said he wouldn't be long."

"Sorry, Padre, I don't have time. My wife's in trouble. I got to find her."

"Patience is a virtue. It will give you strength." Father Bernardus adopted the tone he'd always used when standing at the pulpit. " 'But they that wait upon the Lord shall gain new strength; they shall mount up with wings as eagles; they shall run, and not be weary; and they shall walk, and not faint.' Isaiah 40:31."

Jack kicked himself for having called Terry and arranging a meet. The cop was stringing him along on purpose, no doubt arranging for back up. Jack should never have trusted him. But what choice did he have? He sat.

It had been years since Jack had been inside St. Joseph's. The last time was for his father's funeral. Even then he'd ducked out after Gavin's station house buddies carried in his casket while a lone bagpiper played "Going Home." When Jack was in school and forced to sit through Father Bernardus's endless sermons, he always felt as if his feet were clad in socks filled with angry bees. He would slouch until the pew in front hid him, and then he would slip to the floor and scurry out. Nothing escaped the hawk-eyed priest, though. He would shout Jack's name from the pulpit and would lead off his sermon the next day with the story of the prodigal son.

"What did Terry tell you?" Jack said.

"That you are deeply troubled," Father Bernardus said. "I can offer you the Sacrament of Reconciliation. You can speak freely here. The Lord forgives."

Jack squirmed and looked over his shoulder. "That's not the kind of confession I had in mind, Padre."

"The Lord will be the judge of that." The priest bowed at the crucifix. "How is your old classmate, Geraldo Martinez? We don't see much of him here either."

"Hark? A war hero. Takes care of his grandma. A true American success story. He's got a Better Business Bureau seal hanging in his window, a Mr. Goodwrench diploma on the wall." Jack turned suspicious. "Why do you ask?"

"I am always interested in members of my flock, no matter

how far they have strayed. Geraldo paints automobiles, correct? The kind driven by the street element."

"American classic car enthusiasts. This is California. Everybody's a car nut. There's even a club for mothers who drive minivans. They hold a rally every Saturday. Go from one outlet mall to the next and toast each other with a nonfat caramel macchiato."

"I see you have not outgrown your insolence." Father Bernardus touched his forehead. "I used to blame myself for not being able to reach you and Geraldo. I believed God would deem me a failure as the vessel for His word. I prayed night and day for deliverance. It took years before I finally understood you were my test."

"I'm guessing you didn't get a passing grade."

"There is still plenty of time." The wrinkles deepened on his wizened face as he smiled. "An eternity, actually."

"Don't bet the offering plate on me" Jack looked over his shoulder for Terry again.

"You more than anyone know that gambling is a sin. But in this case, I do favor my odds. Despite the loss of your way, you still know where the True Path lies."

"What makes you say that?"

The priest paused. "You were always an able athlete. I enjoyed watching your feats on the baseball field. You devoted more of your time to sports than classes."

"Play and pray the Catholic way," Jack said impatiently. He dug in his pocket for his phone.

"Our school has a superb sports program now thanks to a very generous sponsor."

The hardness of the pew dug into Jack's tailbone. He tried twisting to relieve it. "You don't say."

"Yes, a benefactor who chooses to remain anonymous. Every year we receive a white envelope delivered by messenger. It contains a cashier's check with the words, Restricted to Sports, in the memo line."

"And you honor it?"

"But of course. We appreciate all of our benefactors and strive to respect their wishes. You'd find the timing of this particular gift interesting. It comes on the same day every year. November 28." The priest paused and placed his hand on Jack's knee. "That is the anniversary of your mother's entry into the Kingdom of Heaven, is it not?"

"I don't know. I forget," Jack said quickly and started to stand. "I got to go. I can't wait around any longer."

Father Bernardus kept his hand on Jack's knee to prevent him from leaving. For an old man, he was surprisingly strong. "That is why I know there is still hope for you, my son. But you must cease wandering in the wilderness and seek redemption. You must ask for God's forgiveness, no matter what sin you may have committed. Ours is a compassionate Heavenly Father. Obey Him and He shall set you free."

"I don't trust my freedom to anybody but me," Jack said.

The priest sighed. "Then let us pray for your deliverance."

He bowed but Jack stared straight ahead. If he thought praying could help protect Katie, he would have done it already.

As soon as Father Bernardus said 'amen' Terry Dolan stepped from the sacristy. "I'll take it from here, Father."

The priest nodded, stood, and made the sign of the cross. Terry dipped his head. When Father Bernardus was gone, the cop joined Jack on the pew. Jack had picked the church for the meet because he was sure Terry wouldn't come in with guns blazing. So far, the detective kept his piece holstered.

"Once an altar boy always an altar boy," Jack said.

"You called me, remember?" Terry said. "You wanted to make a confession about Mai Huntington's murder. You want to insult my faith while you're giving it? Fine. It'll go in the report like everything else. The judge will read it when he's deciding between life in prison and the gas chamber."

A man was moving in the shadows in the east transept. Another took position in the narthex. "I hope the two uniformeds you brought with you remembered to doff their hats," Jack said. "That Carter back there? Looks like the blockhead's biting into an apple he lifted from the homeless box."

Terry leaned forward so he was face-to-face with Jack. "No more games. No more insults. Admit what you did."

"Fine, but hear me out before you do what you got to do. Deal?"

"I'm a cop. I don't make deals with criminals."

"Sure you do. It's how law enforcement works. A cop's got to trade one crime against another if he's going to break the big one that counts. The kind that can make a detective's career."

Terry started to protest but Jack cut him off. "At first, I figured you were on the take when you were parroting Sinclair Huntington. But then I remembered when we were growing up. The Terry Dolan I knew wouldn't take a sip from the bottle of communion wine Hark and I swiped. You're the cop who never forgets to drop a buck in the honor kitty before picking a doughnut out of the squad room box. You wouldn't take a breath of fresh air without checking to make sure it didn't belong to someone else."

"What's that have to do with anything?"

"I'm telling you that I trust you. I need your help."

"Okay, tell me why you killed Mai Huntington and I'll see what I can do. No promises, but they go easier on people who turn themselves in. Why did you do it?"

Jack took a breath. The curtain came up. It was go time. "I didn't. True, I was at the Huntington's mansion the night she died, but I didn't kill her. I'm telling you because I need you to trust me.

I didn't have to tell you I was there. You'd never be able to prove it. There were no witnesses. There's no evidence. There's nothing on the home security system that shows me there. I know because I erased it. I also know whoever killed her erased it before I got there. I checked. It was blank up until the moment I arrived."

"That doesn't prove a thing. You erased yourself killing her," Terry said.

"My guess is the lab rats have already put it through disk analysis and told you the hard drive shows two erasures. Two starts and two stops. Am I right?"

Terry shifted his weight. Jack knew it was a tell. He upped the ante. "I was fishing when I told you Mai had been shot. I knew she hadn't. Someone strong-armed her from behind. Didn't use his hands because there were no finger bruises on her neck. Maybe he meant to choke her a little, scare her some, and it went too far. Or maybe he meant to kill her all along. That would be my bet. Then he pushed her down onto the bed. Mai's neck was snapped, her eyes open to the wall, her shoes still on." Jack paused. "Convinced yet?"

"Nothing you've said proves you didn't kill her. You just gave me enough to haul you in and hold you. Enough so a junior DA fresh out of Hastings Law couldn't fuck it up."

"Do that and you'll let the real killer walk."

"Yeah, and who would that be?" Terry didn't bother to hide his disbelief.

"A con fresh out of Soledad. Caspar Brixton."

The detective shifted his weight again. He'd heard of him. "Why should I believe you?"

Jack went all in. "Because he took Katie. That's why I called you, dammit. He's taken her."

Terry lunged at him. "What have you done?"

Jack twisted out of reach. "Doing what Katie wanted. Come

to you for help. It's why she went and got herself snatched by this guy. She knew I'd have no choice but to call you."

Terry drew his gun and jammed it in Jack's face. "Tell me what you know and tell me fast or so help me."

The cops hiding in the shadows rushed forward. Jack hissed to Terry, "You don't want them to hear this. Call them off. It's the only way we can save Katie."

Terry glared at Jack. Neither blinked. Finally the cop said, "Stand down, men. Resume your positions. That's an order."

The pair retreated to the shadows. Once they were out of earshot, Jack started talking fast. "The night of the gamer gala, I mentioned to Mai Huntington some information I'd come across about her husband. He's bringing in a shipping container full of computer chips under the radar. Mai didn't know anything about it but she should've. She was his chief operating officer. Mai called me the next day. Said she believed he was hiding the super chips from her as a way to keep them off the marital ledger sheet. She was planning to divorce him, and he didn't want to split the new business venture with her fifty-fifty. Just a billionaire doing the same thing Joe Six-Pack does when his marriage blows up. Hides his beer money."

Terry started in. "So she was going to pay you to play private eye, find the chips, and catch Huntington in the act. You went there that night and demanded more money. But she refused, laughed in your face, so you got mad. You tried to scare her, only it went too far."

"No, dammit. Now, listen," Jack shouted.

"No, you listen. What's any of that have to do with Brixton taking Katie? With the murder, for that matter?"

Jack sucked in air. "We don't have much time. Just listen. Brix heard about the chips same as me and is going after them. He blames me for his jolt in Soledad and thinks I owe him. He tried to get me to help him steal the chips but I refused. So he went and found a way to pressure me, namely he went after my family. He sweet-talked Meaghan and now he's got a couple of punks parked out front of her apartment. If I make a move on him, they go in. Then he grabbed Katie's little brother. When I told Katie what happened, she took matters into her own hands. Now Brix's got her too. You wrestled at Saint Joe's. It's a three-point hold and I can't get out of it on my own."

The gun wavered. "Say I believe you. Where's he holding Katie and her brother?"

"I don't know. Katie talked to Meaghan and she must've given her the name of the motel he was holed up in. But forget it. Brix will be long gone because he knows once I found out he took Katie, he better burrow deep."

"And these computer chips? Where are they at?"

"I don't know that either," Jack said. He had to keep a hole card.

"But somebody told you about them, you said so."

"It was scuttle on the street. Big on what they could be worth, short on exactly where they were at."

"The street's no authority."

"You'd be surprised. It passes info faster than Twitter. Besides, Sinclair Huntington confirmed their existence to me."

"You talked to Huntington?" he said, his tone incredulous.

Jack nodded. "But he denied he was bringing them in off the books. Said it was business as usual and Mai had been behind the curve. They're coming, all right, but he wouldn't give me any shipping details. Proprietary information, he said. Huntington's set to debut them at the gamer convention going on at Moscone. He's delivering the keynote."

"You've given me nothing" Terry said and pointed the gun again. "It sounds like one of your cons. You've grown so desperate, now you're trying to drag Katie into your shit."

"I'm telling you the truth. On Katie's life, I swear it. Think about it. That night in the apartment when you pulled on me, I gave you my word I wouldn't tell anyone and ruin your career and I never did. You know why? Because of Katie. It's the same thing now. I give you my word because of her."

Terry's piece wavered again. Jack swallowed. It tasted bitter. "This is real. Katie's in trouble. Come on, Terry. You loved her once. You probably still do. Do it for her. Help me."

Terry hesitated and then nodded. "Okay, for her."

Jack shoulders slumped. "Thanks, man."

"It's not going to be easy. I can't put an APB on Brixton. He'd kill Katie and her brother for sure."

"Brix won't do anything to them as long as he thinks he can still get me to lead him to the computer chips," Jack said. "He can't give up that leverage."

"How are you going to find them? Sinclair Huntington? He's not going to say if he has something to hide. And there's no way I could get a court order to force him to talk. No judge or politician in town would ever cross him."

"I have ways to find the chips, all right," Jack said. "And when I do, we can use them as bait to lure Brix. As soon as he makes his move, you bust him and force him to release Katie."

Terry shook his head. "My captain would never give me authorization to work with you. He'd yank my badge just for asking."

"Okay, I'll set up a play. You don't need to know anything about it. When Brix shows, I call you. You just happen to receive an anonymous tip and make the bust of the year."

Terry didn't look so sure. "What makes you think Brix would fall for it?"

"Because I'm good at what I do. Because Katie's life depends on me being the best con artist in the world."

"I can't stand down on this. A murder's been committed. Two

people have been abducted. You're planning a crime. I can't stand down. You know I can't."

"I'm not asking you to," Jack said. "All I'm asking is you to wait on it a couple of hours. In the meantime you keep gathering information from the murder scene. There's got to be something there that links Brix. He let it slip that he knew Mai's neck had been broken. How would he know that unless he was there? You can also level the playing field. Send those Mounties lurking in the shadows to my sister's and have them roust those punks parked out front. Brix will chalk it up to bad luck. That's one less hostage we have to worry about."

Terry took his time thinking it over. Jack's skin felt on fire while he waited. Finally the cop spoke. "Okay, we'll try it your way. But if it turns out you've been playing me, I won't stop until I put you down."

"You won't have to," Jack said. "If this goes south, someone will have already beat you to it."

27

It was late and San Francisco Bay was upside-down night. The lights from the Bay Bridge twinkled on the inky water. Bioluminescent wakes churned by ships mimicked slow-moving comets. Few people walked along the Embarcadero at this hour. Jack kept his head down as he neared Pier 22½. The door to Station House 35's truck bay was closed, the upstairs windows in the fire fighters' bunk room yellow from night-lights. It was all he could do to keep from banging on the door and demanding entrance. But he couldn't bring Marquis Williams into the play no matter how much he needed him. Jack had to resist giving in to the thought of Brix terrorizing Katie. He had to stay in control and so he kept on walking.

The sidewalk blackened as it reached the underbelly of the Bay Bridge. Next to the span's anchoring tower was a sagging chain link fence. The homeless had pulled it loose. Jack ducked through a gap.

A narrow catwalk ran atop the bulwark and he followed it the way he came, using the fence to screen him from the street. He was careful of his footing, as a misstep would send him plunging into the water or onto the jagged splinters of rotting pylons. Wharf rats scurried ahead as he inched along. A roosting seagull screeched and clacked its bill. Jack didn't screech back.

Pier 24 stood between him and the dock where the *Phoenix* was moored. The pier's converted warehouse was home to a private collection of photographs that was open to the public on a limited basis. Jack had visited a few times, drawn by its gallery of mug shots from the 1930s and 1940s. There was an Okie who'd turned to robbing banks when he lost his farm to one. A gun moll who believed she should have more choices in life than being a wife, a waitress, or a whore. A smalltime grifter who was outgrifted by the big boys on Wall Street. Jack would study each face and the lesson was always the same. It wasn't don't get greedy and it wasn't don't get caught. It was the rich and powerful are rich and powerful.

A night watchman sat inside a dimly lit hut. He was either cooping or watching reruns of *The Golden Girls* on a portable TV that was stashed beneath the desk because his shoulders were slumped and his chin buried in his chest. Jack sneaked past him and circled the warehouse and reached the other side.

Two hundred yards of cold, black water separated him from the *Phoenix*. He could swim across if he had to. Bay water temperature was in the fifties and as long as he kept his head and didn't panic, he'd be fine. But if he started floundering, the cold would suck his energy in minutes and he'd be no better off than the lost souls who somehow survived the big walk off the bridge only to have the shock of hypothermia and pull of the tide finish the job.

Fear was healthy. It could keep a person from doing something really dumb, like stealing when the odds of getting caught were surefire or when the punishment far exceeded the payoff. The worst time to let fear take over was when your life depended on keeping your cool. His father taught him the lesson the hard way.

Back when Jack was at St. Joseph's, Father Bernardus had caught him running a Ponzi on the other students and suspended him for a week. Vowing to teach his son a lesson, Gavin drove Jack to an old burned-out cinderblock building in the Bayview. The fire department used it for training rookies. He had Jack dress in a bunker coat and pants and put on a respirator and mask.

"You think you know it all, do you?" Gavin said, slamming a helmet on Jack's head and hammering it with his fist. "We'll see about that, boyo."

They entered a dark and narrow stairwell and began climbing. By the third floor, Jack was breathing hard and swimming with sweat. The air tank dug into his shoulder blades and the weight of it pulled his neck until it ached. They kept going until he lost count of how many floors they climbed. Finally, Gavin opened a door on a landing and led him to a windowless room with concrete walls as black as cinder. A stink that smelled like a burning tire made Jack's eyes water.

"Sit down and catch some wind," his dad told him. "You're going to need it."

Jack collapsed on a metal bench, his chest heaving, his sides burning. "Don't worry about me," he said between gasps. "I can take whatever you can dish."

Gavin grinned. "You think so, do you?" Then he threw a switch.

Motors whirred and fans blew and the room quickly filled with choking clouds of oily black smoke. Jack yanked his respirator mask over his nose and mouth and started sucking hard. Nothing. No air at all.

"Damn," he thought and fumbled for the valve that would start the flow of oxygen.

By the time he got it going, he was choking and lightheaded. Now flames were shooting out of burners that ringed the bottom of the walls. Within seconds the room was hotter than a Christmas oven. Jack's fingernails felt like embers. He jumped up and ran for the door that would lead him into the rat's maze and the stairwell beyond.

"What's your hurry?" his old man said, blocking his path.

"Get out of my way," Jack shouted into his oxygen mask, not sure if the words could be heard or not.

Gavin laughed crazily and stuck out his foot. Jack tripped and went sprawling. When he tried to get up, a big, heavy boot pinned him.

"Stay low, if you want to breathe. You're going to have to crawl."

The weight of the boot lifted. Jack twisted around. His father was gone. Jack tried to move but couldn't. It was as if his bunker coat and pants had melted to the sooty floor.

"Okay, I'm sorry," Jack screamed into the mask. "Do you hear me? I'm sorry. I won't do it again. Now turn off the flames."

There was no response.

Jack pulled the mask away from his face. "Did you hear me? I said I'm sorry."

Still no response. The heat grew hotter, searing his throat as he shouted. "Help. Help."

The hiss of flames was the only response. The choice was clear: Give in to fear and die or save himself. Jack pushed off the floor and ran. He stayed as low as he could and crashed through the wall of flames. He groped for the opening to the hallway and plunged ahead. Finally, he found the metal door to the stairwell. Jack twisted the handle. It didn't budge.

"No," he shouted.

He yanked again. Nothing. He put his shoulder into it. An alarm started screaming. His air tank was running dry. A window beckoned at the end of the hall. Jack ran to it. It was screened by a thick mesh of heavy-gauge steel. Freedom was five floors below. So was death if he chose to jump. Jack ran back to the door, raised his foot, and brought the heel of his boot smashing down on the handle. The lock snapped and the handle turned. He yanked the door open as his air ran out. Jack took the stairs three at a time.

He collapsed to the ground when he got outside and lay there sucking in sweet fresh air in big, deep gulps. Gavin stood there watching. The look on his face was a mixture of pride and disapproval. "You may be tough, boyo, but it's knowing when to fight and knowing when to run that'll save you."

It was time to fight, Jack knew. He stared across the black water to the *Phoenix* but didn't jump in. During previous visits to the photo gallery, he had noticed the rich collector stored a kayak on his private pier so he could take morning paddles along the waterfront. Jack took the kayak and stroked across the water. He tied to the *Phoenix's* bowline and climbed on board.

The door to the fireboat's bridge was unlocked. The last thing a fire fighter wanted when answering a call was to play Where Are My Keys. Jack entered the wheelhouse, grabbed a slicker from a hook, and threw it over the computer screen mounted to the chart table. He stuck his head under the makeshift hood.

The computer came alive with a tap of a key and the home screen had a shortcut to the port's manifest database. Jack clicked on it. A window popped up asking for a user ID and password. Guessing the ID was easy. *Phoenix*. The password stumped him. He slipped from under the slicker and searched the chart table for a strip of paper with a name on it. Nothing. He knew better than to guess. He shined his penlight around for inspiration. Marquis' basset hound stared out from a snapshot tacked above the helm. Jack remembered the dog. Marquis always said he had the soul of a poet. Jack ducked beneath the slicker and typed in Langston Hughes. He was in.

The search function took him directly to the *Sincerity's* manifest. It was organized alphanumerically by serial shipping container code. Jack narrowed the search by plugging in two eights, then three eights, and then four. Of the 9,000 TEUs on board the inbound freighter, only one had two double eights in its eleven-digit code. He clicked on the entry and another pop-up opened. The listing described the container's contents as ceramic tiles being shipped by White Tiger of the West Ltd. to Triangulum.

For the first time in a long while, Jack managed a grin. "What's up, pussycat?"

28

The eastern span of the Bay Bridge resembled a cruise ship and dark waters roiled beneath as the sky above paled with a new morning. Hark was behind the wheel of the '64 Impala lowrider.

"Like old times, eh *'mano*? Saddled up and ready to ride. Rescuing a damsel in distress, no less. And a mighty fine one too. All due respect."

"Katie wants me to have faith that she knows what she's doing going after Brix, but I got to tell you this is taking marital trust a little too far," Jack said.

"If anybody can handle herself, she can. Katie's tough. I watched a clip on her website of her leading a step class. Half the time she's doing these kick-ass kickboxing moves. You got to be in some shape do that for an hour or so. Once we take care of this Brix *cabron*, I'm going sign up. Got to take off a few of the *LB*s I put on sitting behind a desk."

Hark switched lanes for the Maritime exit. "Run it down again, what we doing going to Oaktown when you're pretty sure he's got Katie stashed somewhere else?"

"We're going to do a little longshoring," Jack said.

"You mean like *On the Waterfront*? Cool. I watched it the other night on Netflix. Who you think I'm like? The Lee J. Cobb heavy or Brando?"

"As many times your nose been broken? I'd say the actor played the preacher, Karl Malden."

"*Chingame*," Hark said. "Dude harped more than Father Bernardus."

The Port of Oakland had twenty deepwater berths and thirty-five container cranes spread across twelve hundred acres. Hark had his work cut out steering through a maze of containers stacked six high and dodging forklifts, big rigs and trains, but they finally pulled up to Berth 23 without so much as a scratch in the lowrider's hand-buffed paint job.

"What a rust bucket," Hark said. He parked so they had a view of the *Sincerity*. "Captain's got no respect for his ride."

Reddish-brown streaks ran from the white-hulled freighter's scuppers to the waterline. Ropes green with algae and thick as elephant trunks moored the scow to its berth. Two cranes plucked TEUs off the deck and deposited them in stacked rows on the dock or straight onto flatbed trailers hooked to carry container trucks.

"Huntington sent his diamonds in a rough box, all right. He's hoping Customs and his competitors won't look too closely," Jack said.

"I was expecting big, burly dudes singing sea chanteys and swinging hooks," Hark said.

"Time is money. Those cranes can unload a cargo ship in a few hours instead of a few days like it used to take."

Hark drummed his fingers on the chrome chain link steering wheel. "You ever get the feeling we'll all wind up being replaced by machines one day?"

"Adapt or die."

"They teach you that in college?"

"No, man, I learned it on the streets."

"So which of those big tin cans is filled with the chips?"

"Seek and ye shall find."

Jack pulled out his tablet. He'd downloaded a standard supply chain logistics app for tracking regular serial shipping container codes, and Leonard's app. He tapped on the standard one and keyed in the code number with the four eights. The screen filled with a map of the Port of Oakland and he zoomed in on the blinking dot.

"Huntington's container is still on board. The ship's tracker won't update its location until the code gets wanded by a hand scanner again. They'll do that as it's being off-loaded."

"What are we going do then? Chain it to the back of my whip and tow it home?"

"No, we'll play post office," Jack said.

"We could do it the old-fashioned way, jack its ass." Hark motioned toward the Beretta M9 fast-holstered beneath his bucket.

"Too dangerous. Truckers working the waterfront pack because of hijackings, and then there's local law. Besides, I want Brix to take it."

Hark swiveled his head, his neck tat stretching as he checked the rearview and side mirrors. "You think he's here?"

"I'm counting on it. It's all part of the play now."

"But I had my eye glued to the rearview the whole drive over. Nobody tailed us. I'd bet my *abuela's* restaurant on it."

"He's been here for a while. I've been giving it some thought; how he's been a step ahead. Somebody's feeding him information."

"You mean the Fangs?"

"Couldn't be. Jimmie and his dad hired Brix as an insurance policy, but they never knew the details of the shipment."

"Then who?"

"Someone on the inside."

Jack switched to Leonard's 3-D QR tracker app and plugged in the serial number of the container Leonard believed was part of Big Angel's test. It was still on board the *Sincerity* too.

"Show time," Jack said, pulling on a ball cap with the San Francisco Fire Department logo on it.

THE TABLET and his father's gold badge pinned to a dark blue shirt completed Jack's uniform as he climbed the *Sincerity's* gangplank. He was greeted stiffly by the first mate who escorted him to the top floor of the bridge castle.

Jack pointed to the tablet's screen that flashed a ginned up form with *Sincerity* typed at the top and another screen of the ship's deck plan, which he downloaded off the net. "Firefighting equipment inspection," he told the captain. "Yeah, you're in Oakland but San Francisco FD's in charge of all the ports."

"No need for inspection," he said, his English halting, but his authority and annoyance loud and clear. "Sprinkler system A-OK. All extinguishers got official stamp. I show you log."

Jack waved the tablet. "I got digital copies of your paperwork right here, Skip, but Code 162, Section 34 requires spot inspections. I don't make the rules; I just carry them out. You want to convince Chief Garcia otherwise, be my guest." He whipped out his phone. "She'll be happy to give you an answer. I got to warn you, though, she's more pit bull than dalmatian. Could cost you a couple extra days in port while she's thinking it over, plus what the Port'll charge you for additional dock fees, not to mention whatever your customers will ding you for late delivery." Jack cocked a brow. "Does that come out of your wages?"

The captain wasn't budging so Jack delivered the *coup de grâce*. "Of course, the department's budget is under review and

Chief Garcia is busy making a case for adding new personnel. I wouldn't be surprised if she ordered me to test your sprinkler lines and equipment for leaks while I'm here to prove a point. What do you got, a couple miles of water pipe crisscrossing the decks, another few thousand feet of hose? Now we're talking real overtime."

The captain scowled and then barked an order at the first mate. Jack didn't need to understand a word to know he'd been handed the run of the ship. The first mate escorted him off the bridge and handed him over to a deckhand with orders to dog Jack.

The ship was nearly a quarter mile long. The TEUs were stacked six high above deck and six deep below. As Jack crossed the main deck he kept an eye on the cranes swinging twenty-five-ton containers overhead. One slip of a cable and there wouldn't be anything left of him but a smear to hose off. He rechecked the manifest database. Huntington's container was placed under deck midship. He toggled the screen with the *Serenity's* deck map and located a stairway that led to a narrow passageway. It was dark and dank and lit by dim bulbs protected by steel cages. The deckhand stayed hot on his heels.

Halfway down Jack ran into a watertight door. An iron wheel the size of steering wheel was the knob. He cranked it. It didn't budge. He turned to the deckhand. "How about some help here?"

The deckhand didn't move a muscle so Jack gripped the wheel again and put his back into it as he thought about Katie, thought about where she was at. Finally, the wheel began to give. The door pushed open with a loud screech that made his fillings hurt. He shined a flashlight into the ship's bowels. Though the *Serenity* was docked, its great engines were idling, which caused the hull to throb and shudder.

Thick black exhaust and nauseating diesel fumes filled the

gloomy hold. It was enormous and divided into bays. The big metal shipping boxes had been loaded lengthwise into fixed vertical racks and stacked in tiers. Each bay had a yellow sign with black numbers and the rows were marked the same way, only with letters. Jack followed a maze-like route to Bay 9, Row D. The TEUs were stacked with their swinging double rear doors facing out to display their serial shipping container codes. He started with the bottom container and worked up, checking the numbers as he went. Double double-eights was the second from the top.

A fire sprinkler nozzle hung above the tier and Jack gestured to the deckhand that he was going to use the vertical rack's built-in ladder to inspect it. The ladder was coated with grease and he slipped twice as he climbed, nearly knocking his teeth out when his chin smacked into the rungs. He pulled even to the top of the container with the chips and pretended to fumble with his flashlight. The lens shattered when it hit the hard deck below. The deckhand swore. Jack returned a sheepish grin and then mimed for him to fetch another light. The sailor appeared relieved to get out of the line of fire.

As soon as he was out of sight, Jack slipped on a head lamp and went to work, pulling a new sequence of stick-on numbers from his pocket and slapping them over the original serial code. Then he affixed a 3-D QR transponder directly above it. He executed a perfect fireman's slide down the ladder and tapped the app on the tablet. His queen of hearts was ready to play.

Jack had to move fast now to keep a step ahead. Any one of the other containers could serve as a black king, but Jack had a special one in mind. It was filled with contents that had caught his attention when he was searching the *Sincerity's* manifest. He found it in the next bay and changed its serial code with new stick-on numbers so it now sported Huntington's lucky double double-eights. He had his king of clubs.

Jack checked his watch, wondering what was taking the deckhand so long. No matter, he still had one last card to mark. He tapped the tablet and logged in a new set of numbers into Leonard's app. The location of the control container for Big Angel's supposed test run started flashing. His king of spades was filled with thousands of notebooks that had become that season's must have gadget. It was stacked at the other end of the ship, but Jack had everything he needed right where he stood. He clicked on the app's dashboard and adjusted the container's pickup and delivery instructions. The app flashed confirmation.

Street hustlers called dealing three-card monte "tossing the broad" and while Katie would surely object to such a sexist term, Jack knew her life depended on just how well he could throw the bitch. It was time to deal. He retraced his steps through the maze of tiered bays. As he came around a corner, the deckhand approached. His cap was pulled low and he was holding the flashlight by his side. Only it wasn't turned on. And it wasn't a flashlight.

29

Despite the foul air and gloom, Brix's pupils were the size of pinpricks. The gun jumped in his hand as he pointed it at Jack. "Surprise, shithead."

Jack feigned shock. "How did you get here?"

Brix sneered. "You're so fucking lame you never saw me coming. All this time, I been stuck to your ass like toilet paper."

Jack gave a nervous twitch. "Hey, I'm doing my job like I said. The Fangs wanted me to find their chips and I did. I double-checked. It's the right container all right. You can tell Jimmie yourself and collect whatever it is they're paying you as insurance. I don't want a cent. I just want Katie and her brother back."

Brix laughed. "You think I'd give the Fangs anything? I don't take orders from chinks."

Jack went for wide-eyed. "You're not going to tell them about the ship?"

"And give up this big of a score?" Brix waved his gun at the stacks of TEUs. "You're as stupid as those fucking raghead pirates hijacking ships in Africa. What do they get? A boatload of fifty-five-inch hi-def TVs for their mud huts, and they don't even got electricity."

Fresh blood stained the deckhand's cap now perched on Brix's head. "What did you do to him?" Jack asked.

"What's it matter?"

"If he doesn't report in, they'll lock the ship down tight while they look for him. They make this as a crime scene, how long do you think it'll take before they find us?"

Brix sneered. "Rats have been jumping ship since the pilgrims. You take a guy lives in a rathole in some rat-hole country, eating nothing but rice, and then show him what we got here? They all would jump give them half a chance. Not that I'd let them, if I had my way. Lock the borders tight and shoot them on sight, that's my motto."

Jack nodded at the tattoos on his forearms. "I can see who you shared pruno with in prison."

"Fucking *A* right. The Brothers are real Americans."

"The ship's got video surveillance," Jack said. "They'll nail you for murder."

"Ah, don't be such a pussy. The dink took a little fall down the stairs. He'll wake up with a headache, won't remember a thing." Brix jabbed the gun so the tip was an inch from Jack's nose. "But there's no cameras down here so quit stalling. Which one of these boxes has the chips? And don't try bullshitting me. Remember who's holding your pretty little wife." He stuck out his tongue and licked the air.

Jack thought about going for the gun. He was faster than Brix and could snatch it away and shove it down his throat. But no matter how hard he pistol-whipped him, Brix would never tell where Katie and Brad were. He wasn't the first person Jack had run into with nothing left to lose.

"Over here." He led Brix to the king of clubs.

Brix studied the tier, his eyes stopping at the container now sporting double double-eights. "How do you know that's it?"

"Each box has a serial number. They're like fingerprints. This one matches the ship's manifest."

"Yeah, how did you get hold of that?"

"It's computerized. I hacked it."

"You think you're pretty smart."

Jack shrugged. "Well, like you said, who's holding the gun? Who's holding my wife?"

"Exactly." Brix laughed. "Open it so I can make sure it's the right box."

"See that padlock? Those wire seals with tags? If we mess with those, Customs will notice when it's being off-loaded. Then the only place it'll be going to is to the Fed's warehouse for inspection. We got to leave it be until it's off the ship."

Brix rubbed his jaw with the gun's barrel. "Okay, smart guy, what's your plan for taking it once it's off the boat?"

"I never made one. My job was to find the chips. That's all."

"No con, no game?" Brix shook his head. "That's not your style, McCoul."

Jack shrugged. Brix kept the gun pointed as he pulled out a phone and snapped a picture of the container's serial code. Then he punched in a number and hit send. Ten seconds later Brix's phone pinged. He nodded as he read the incoming text.

"Okay, it's the real McCoy. I can't say I'm not disappointed. As much as I want the chips, I was really hoping you'd try and bluff me. Give me a reason to shoot you in the head and shove your ass in a container and send you off to Timbuktuistan. Then go back and enjoy the spoils. Your wife. Your sister." Brix licked the air again.

Jack fought the urge to leap across the narrow passageway and smash Brix's head into the steel wall of containers. He nodded at the phone. "Looks like you got access to the shipping manifest too."

Brix showed his corn-kernel teeth. "You know your problem?

You always overestimate the risk and underestimate the other players. It's why you're small time. Always have been, always will be."

"Okay, you win. You got what you wanted. The container's all yours. You can do with it whatever you want. I don't care; it's not my business. Now let Katie and Brad go. Ease up on Meaghan."

"Sure. No problem." Brix gave a jack-o'-lantern grin. "As soon as I got the chips off this tub and check them out. I don't trust you. Hell, I don't even trust myself most of the time."

~

JACK RETURNED to the Impala to watch the Serenity finish unloading. The gigantic cranes moved as if choreographed, plucking containers from the deck and placing them on waiting trucks.

"It go down like you wanted?" Hark asked as Jack slipped into the shotgun seat.

"More or less. Brix made his play for the container."

"That was a bold move. He could've taken you out once he IDed it."

"Yeah, but Brix is feral enough to always be on guard for a last minute switch. He needs me alive until he's able to open the box. At least that's what I was betting on."

Hark nodded. "Betting with your life, you mean. On account of Katie and her brother."

"Family," Jack said. "What you going do?"

Hark tipped his Locs as he watched the containers being off-loaded. "Most of these boxes got numbers on the sides as well as on the back doors. You said you only changed the ones on the rear. Isn't Brix going catch that?"

"Not right away. Even the loading crews don't bother cross-checking the numbers. They're looking at thousands of TEUs going by in an hour. They don't have time to compare the side numbers with the door numbers. That would take an extra step, plus the serial codes are too long to memorize."

"You sure?"

Jack nodded. "Leo, the kid who built the transponder app, did a whole study on it. It's a big selling point for his product."

Jack balanced the tablet on his lap and tracked the three containers. The king of clubs was the first to be scanned, hoisted, and off-loaded. A waiting carry container truck with a soaring eagle painted on the cab doors was called into position by the terminal operator as the container now coded as Huntington's was being lowered. The crane deposited the big metal box onto its empty trailer with a clang and as soon as its cables were rewinding, the Eagle Express truck took off.

"Looks like it's getting an escort," Hark said.

A new black Yukon with the dealer tags still on it swung out from behind a stack of dockside containers and took position behind the truck as it sped toward the freeway.

"That'll be Ruddy Face and the winch monkeys," Jack said.

"Cutler, right? Brix's inside man. You called that right."

Jack nodded. "I ran down all the possibilities of who could be giving Brix the 411. There was something Henri Le Conte told me—how Brix would steal sailboats. I checked Sinclair Huntington's sailing race team website. It had bios of his yacht crew, their hometowns listed. Guess what? Old Ruddy Face grew up in Sausalito too."

"Definitely not Scientologists," Hark said with a laugh.

A few seconds later a white Mercedes fell in line behind. "And that would be Brix."

"Dude picked himself an expensive ride just being out of the joint. Doesn't exactly tell his PO he's on the straight and narrow and hunting for a nine-to-five."

"Brix thinks subtlety comes in a bag with a string you put in hot water," Jack said. "Run the plates on the Benz and a benjamin to a penny they're lifted."

"Waste of a penny, that bet. Just like we're wasting our time following him, hoping he'll lead us to where he's holding Katie, right?"

Jack nodded. "As much as it's killing me to hold off, I got to play the game on my table in my house according to my rules. I give that up, I lose control."

"Hey, *vato*, remember? It's not my first rodeo either."

The king of spades came off the *Sincerity* next. It was placed onto a carry container truck with a nondescript green cab and no logo on its door. Once loaded, the truck took off for the delivery location Jack had programmed into the 3-D QR. Fifteen minutes later it was the queen of hearts's turn. The container was loaded onto an identical green truck.

Hark fired up the Impala and they followed the chips to San Francisco.

30

Jack sat alone in the loft and reviewed his moves for mistakes. He tried not to picture Katie tied up in a dark room somewhere. It seemed like weeks ago, not days, that Brad had come to him begging for the $50,000. Jack knew he couldn't go backward in life, but that didn't keep him from wishing he'd stuck to his guns.

Telling Brad no had led to a big fight with Katie. Brad accused Jack of signing his death warrant. "These guys will kill me if I don't pay them," he cried and stormed away. Katie insisted that Jack go after him.

Jack refused. "Don't let him guilt-trip you," he told her. "I'm done bailing out your little brother every time he fucks up. He needs to grow up and be responsible for himself."

"We have to give him the money," Katie said. "He promises to pay it back. He says he's through gambling and I believe him. Brad's learned his lesson."

"No," Jack said, his voice rising. "He's just using us. He'll never stop until we say no."

Katie started crying but the more she tried to talk him into it, the more it got Jack's Irish up. He stomped out and went to the

Pier to cool off. It wasn't as if he and Katie never disagreed before, but there was never any winning with her. Even when she did allow that he might be right, Jack always felt like a Neanderthal—the guy looking outside the cave and seeing only one thing. After nursing a few Jamesons, along with his bruised ego, Jack returned home with an apology in mind. He got into bed and before he could get a word out, Katie said she was sorry. Then she launched into a story about when she was a little girl and found a cute baby bird that had fallen out of the nest. She fed it with an eyedropper and kept it in a shoebox lined with tissue. It had pretty feathers and she was sure it was some kind of an exotic species.

"Let me guess," Jack said as they lay there in the dark. "The bird grew up and turned out to be an ordinary pigeon."

She punched his shoulder. "How did you know that?"

"The same way you knew I'd give in and lend Brad the money."

Staring out the window at the bay, Jack wondered if Brix had any little baby birds in his life. Not a chance. Brix was a taker, not a giver. He was the Brad; he was the Meaghan. He was only in it for himself. Brix would do anything, hurt anybody, to get what he thought he deserved. Henri LeConte had told him Brix fed fishhooks to pelicans and probably burned down the family houseboat with his father inside. Knowing that about him didn't scare Jack because it was information he could use. And the more he knew about his opponent, the better Jack liked his odds.

A ringing phone pulled him from his thoughts. It was Jimmie Fang, and he didn't sound happy.

"Where are my chips?" he demanded.

"Why ask me?" Jack said.

"Quit fucking around. Where are they?"

"Hey, Jimmie, if you had trusted me you'd have them by now.

I can't help it if you're having trouble collecting your property. You should've read the fine print in the coverage policy you signed with Brix. He's about as reliable as an insurance company after an earthquake."

"Fang's not laughing. Neither am I."

"You haven't heard from Brix yet?"

"No. Where is he?" Jimmie hissed.

"Last time I saw him he was driving a Mercedes C-Class bumper to bumper with the container truck carrying the smart chips. You got Brix's cell number? Give him a call. Maybe he got a flat tire."

"If I don't get my chips, I'll hold you and your brother responsible."

"Brother. In. Law. Hey, Jimmie, my duty of care ended when you took on Brix and sold me out."

"Brix doesn't make the rules. I do."

"Tell that to your father," Jack muttered.

Jimmie stiffened. "What did you say?"

"I said, somehow I don't think Brix read the user manual."

Jimmie made a sound of air being sucked through closed teeth. "I told you, McCoul, I'm holding you responsible. You're going to pay a big price if I don't see my chips. My boys are on their way to your place right now."

"Wake up and smell the latte," Jack said. "Brix took the chips. He never intended to give them to you. He's either going to sell them on the black market himself or he signed with another team with deeper pockets. Do the math. Whose are bottomless?"

The phone grew silent except for the chirping of birds in the background. "Fang won't be happy," Jimmie finally said.

"Fathers. What you going do?" Jack let it hang for a bit. "Tell you what. And I'm trusting you big time here. Brix is screwing you and he's trying to screw me too. He grabbed Katie and Brad, thinking he can force me to stand down. Call off your soldiers for a bit. Give me a little time to work things out and I'll get your chips and save you and your old man face."

"Why would you do that for us?"

"Call it mutual interest. And if I'm successful and you want to show your appreciation for good service? Well, don't feel like you have to wait til Christmas."

"And me and my soldiers sit by?"

"I can't have you going in shooting everybody. You got to trust me."

"For how long?"

"Not long. Be patient."

"Patients are in hospitals," Jimmie said. "If I don't get my chips, you won't need one."

Jack didn't wait for the little gangster to say another word. He clicked off and counted the seconds going by because he was betting Katie's life on the next call.

It finally came. Caller ID said it was Katie's cell but she wasn't on the other end. He let it ring until it was about to roll to voice mail before picking up.

"Top o' the mornin', don't you know?" he answered.

"You're a dead man," Brix hissed. "Your wife, she's already dead. Her brother? Dead. You're all dead. Are you laughing now?"

Jack could see the look on Brix's face when he snapped the lock on what he thought was the double double-eights container and swung open the doors only to find boxes of Chinese-made Saint Patrick's Day decorations. Boxes of pinup posters of leprechauns advertising Guinness and paper chains of shiny shamrocks.

Jack kept his voice calm. "With $100 million worth of smart chips to help me get over my grief? Yeah, I think I'll be able to learn how to laugh again just fine."

Brix sputtered. "You're bluffing."

"There's one way to find out."

"I'm not playing your game. You blew it big time."

"The cards have been dealt. The pot's on the table. Are you calling or stalling?"

There was silence for a long while. "You wouldn't 've answered the phone if you didn't want to make a deal," Brix said. "Chips for your family, right? Okay I'll ante up. Bring me the real container."

"Not before I speak to Katie. Put her on."

It took an achingly long time but then Jack heard a click. "Hello?" she said, her voice tentative.

"Hey, babe. How's he treating you?"

"Oh, I'm fine. I've been doing Transcendental Meditation. I'd tell you where we are but they told me not to. One of them is pointing a pistol at Brad."

Her pronouns weren't lost on Jack. "How's he doing?"

"His equilibrium is off. I tried to get Brad to do some yoga to get centered, but he won't listen. I'm worried about him."

Jack filed away his brother-in-law's condition too. "This will be over soon. I promise. Hang in there, okay?"

Brix cut her off. "Satisfied? Now bring me what belongs to me."

"Other way around," Jack said. "You deliver Katie and Brad to me and I'll give you the container."

"Funny guy. That's not the way this is going to work."

Monte was like real estate. It was all about location, location, location. "Sure it is," Jack said. "Here's the address and the time. Don't be early; don't be late. And, Brix, don't forget to bring your own truck driver. You bought it; you haul it."

31

"I feel better if you let me put some of my low lows up in the rafters," Hark said as he eyeballed the warehouse's high ceilings. "We're sitting ducks here."

"No shooters," Jack said. "I'm not going to risk Katie getting caught in a crossfire."

"What about us?"

"We're professionals."

Hark chewed on that a bit. "Okay, the Bronze Star and Purple Heart Uncle Sam pinned on my chest said I can handle someone pulling on me and not wet my pants, but first guy pops a cap? I'm going pop right back." He motioned toward the Beretta hidden beneath the tails of his long-sleeved flannel. "It's about respect."

They were sitting on folding metal chairs around a beat up worktable in a building made of reinforced red bricks. It doubled as a parking garage during Giant's games. The guy who owned it owed Jack for helping him out when a developer tried to pull a fast one and cheat him out of his property. A green truck hooked to a carry trailer with a shipping container on its back was parked next to them.

"You pretty sure this is going play the way you planned it?" Hark asked.

Jack shrugged. "Pretty sure. If not, well, we'll have to improvise."

"Improvise, huh. What? Slap them with a dictionary?"

"Something like that."

"Speaking of cops, you call our old Saint Joe's buddy?" Hark asked.

"Terry? Yeah, but just to make sure he'd gotten rid of those punks at Meaghan's. She's safe. Terry had her and the kids driven up to Ukiah where we got a cousin."

"But you didn't tell him where we're at."

"Brix spent too much time inside. He can smell the shine on a cop's shoes a mile away. Soon as it's Terry's turn in the play, I'll hit the speed dial."

"You got your wife's old boyfriend on your favorites? *'Mano,'mano.*"

The bay door to the warehouse was open to the street and a black Yukon with dealer tags followed by a white Mercedes pulled in. Cutler and a winch monkey jumped out of the front seat of the SUV and started sweeping the warehouse. They checked under the truck and trailer.

"Clear," Cutler yelled.

"Dude watches too many cop shows," Hark said.

The driver's door of the Mercedes opened and Brix stepped out. He grinned smugly. "If we'd worked this thing from the start together like I asked, we wouldn't be having this problem."

"Problem? What problem?" Jack said. "All I see is a business transaction."

"Those the chips?" Brix poked his chin at the TEU on the green carry container truck.

"That my wife and her brother in the Yukon?" Jack asked.

"Show me the chips."

"Show me my wife."

Brix thought about it and then laughed. "Why not?" He motioned to Cutler. The weather-beaten sailor opened the back door of the Yukon. The second winch monkey was sitting between Katie and Brad. "Satisfied?"

"Bring them out. Let them stretch their legs," Jack said.

Brix gave the okay. Cutler yanked out Katie. Her hands were bound with a zip tie, her mouth gagged by a scarf. The winch monkey came next. He had a gun in one hand and dragged Brad with the other. Brad was zip tied and gagged too. Jack rolled his shoulders. Breathed in, breathed out. He wanted to leap across the warehouse, grab Brix around his neck, and snap it like Mai's had been snapped. But he didn't. Whenever he was dealing monte, he never showed anything he didn't want the mark to see. No one had ever been able to spot his tell.

Jack blew Katie a kiss. She looked as calm as dawn. "Just a little bit longer, babe," he said.

Brix's grin spread. "Tell me, McCoul. How's it feel to be on the losing end."

"Unfamiliar. Let's get this over. Go ahead and check the container and then take it out of here."

"Sure." Brix waited, dragging it out. "Just as soon as you say you lost and I won. Go ahead. I want to hear you say it. Say it front of your wife and our homeboy here." He crossed his arms, his prison tats growing taut.

"*Chingate,* racist motherfucker," Hark said. "I'm full-blood Mexican American and proud of it. You can call me Latino, *cholo,* former misguided youth or Corporal Geraldo Martinez, US Army, Retired, but no way no how not never your homie."

Brix bared his pointy yellow teeth but Jack quickly put a hand up. "Okay, Brix. You won. I lost. You beat me. Satisfied?"

"You hear that, sweet piece?" Brix said. "Your hubby's a fucking loser. A small-timer who never had what it takes to play with the big boys." He pointed at the container. "Go ahead. Open it."

The winch monkey took a pair of heavy-duty bolt cutters and snipped the padlock, his biceps bulging from the effort. Next, he cut the customs seal. Cutler joined him and they swung open the double doors to reveal a wall of cardboard boxes stamped, White Tiger of the West, Ltd. The monkey wrestled out a box. Cutler slit the top with a box cutter and then turned the opened box upside down. Ceramic tiles spilled out.

"Those are in case Customs inspected the container," Brix said. "Get a box from the next row."

The monkey cleared the way to get at the second row of boxes. He handed a box to Cutler who slit it and folded back the cardboard wings. Shiny black microchips gleamed from a bed of protective foam. A lopsided grin added more creases to his face. "Bingo," Cutler said.

Brix scurried over. "Open another." The monkey unloaded a second box from the same row. It was packed with chips. "And another." Brix panted with excitement. He pumped his fist and gloated at Jack. "Winning's not everything; it's the only thing. And I just won the fucking lottery."

Jack shrugged and then made a point of stealing a glance at the serial code on the container door. "Satisfied? Now load up and get out." He started to walk over to untie Katie.

"Hold it right there," Brix shouted.

32

Brix studied the serial code on the container door and the photo on his phone, trying to figure it out. The sequence of numbers was wrong while the serial code on the container filled with Saint Paddy's Day crap had been right. He glanced at Jack and then at the code.

"Cutler," he shouted. "See to McCoul's wife. If he takes another step toward her, do your thing."

Cutler changed places with the winch monkey guarding Katie and put his arm around her neck. His biceps weren't as overdeveloped as the winch winder twins, but they bulged all the same. Katie didn't bat a long, silky lash. She seemed as relaxed as she did when she did deep breathing after yoga or sex. Not Brad. He slumped onto the floor. Even the gag couldn't muffle his moans.

"You or the Mex makes a move, Cutler snaps her neck," Brix said. He switched the phone for his gun, pointing it at Jack and Hark. He shouted at the twins. "Check those numbers. Do it fast."

They dragged the table to the container. One of the monkeys

hopped up and stood on it. "There's numbers stuck on numbers like the container full of shamrock shit," he said.

"Peel them off," Brix hissed.

The stick-ons revealed the hidden serial code beneath. There wasn't an eight to be seen.

Brix nodded, the barrel of the gun jumping as he did. "Climb in the container and check the next row."

The winch monkeys went to work. They pulled out more boxes to clear a way through the second row and then grabbed a box from the third. They ripped it open. "It's full of fucking tiles," they said in unison.

Brix stared at the opening that had been made in the third row. It was as black as a missing tooth, nothing behind it but the empty throat of the container.

"Fuck," he screamed. He grabbed the cutter that had been left next to the opened boxes and stalked over to Jack. With the gun in one hand, he held the blade so that it caught the light angling from a skylight and slashed the air. "You think I never played monte before? Never tossed the cunt myself?" He slashed close to Jack's face. "You marked the cards. Where's the third container at? Tell me or Cutler breaks her neck. Tell me or I'll shoot her brother and the Mex. Do it or I'll slash your fucking throat, so help me."

Cutler started bringing his fist up, his forearm locking tighter around Katie's neck, the veins in his biceps bulging. Her face turned red. Hark moved his hand toward the tail of his untucked flannel. He could draw and drop Brix, but he didn't have a clean angle on the sunburned sailor.

"Okay, you win." Jack said it loud and fast. "Let her go and I'll show you."

Brix nodded to Cutler but had to shout his name a couple of times to get him to ease up.

Katie took a deep breath and blew it out, just like she did

doing kundalini. Jack walked past the truck and hit a wall switch. An overhead motor whirred and a bay door in the back rolled up. An identical green truck and container was parked on the other side, the cab facing toward an open alley.

Brix fought off a grin. "Check the serial code."

The twins dragged the table over and peeled off a layer of stick-on numbers. "Double eights," Brix crowed. "Let's see if that's my new lucky charm. Open it."

The winch monkeys unlatched the doors to reveal a wall of boxes stamped 'White Tiger of the West, Ltd.' They slid one out and peeled back the top folds. Shiny black microchips winked back.

"Check another," Brix said, still brandishing the gun and the box cutter.

The next box was packed with chips too. So was a third.

Brix brayed, "That's what I'm talking about. Put them back and collect the boxes McCoul salted the other container with. Don't leave a single chip behind. Not a fucking one."

Brix grinned at Jack. "That was fucking amateur hour. How'd you ever get the rep you got?"

Jack shrugged. "You can't fault a guy for trying."

Brix shadowboxed then raised his hands in triumph. "Against me? You never stood a chance."

"Probably not," Jack said. "But I'm not your problem. Jimmie Fang and his dad are. They already know you're going to keep the chips. They won't give you a pass. They'll do whatever it takes to save face."

Brix spit on the floor. "Chinks like them? They ought to be glad to be living in this country. They don't like it; they can go the fuck back where they came from."

"This dude for real?" Hark muttered.

"And Huntington? You think he's not going to turn the world upside down searching for you and the chips?" Jack pointed to

Cutler, who was still standing behind Katie. Brad was slumped at their feet. "Hunting down Ruddy Face over there? What he did to Mai?"

"I told you don't call me that," Cutler said.

Brix brayed again. "You still don't get it. It's a wonder you got anywhere in the life. You don't see shit."

The curtain opened all the way and Jack finally saw everything. He'd always seen the different pieces, not always so clearly and never all fitted together, but enough to put the play together the way he did.

"You mean, did I know Huntington's been pulling the levers the whole time?" Jack shrugged. "Maybe not at first, but who else could it be? When he found out who was making the chips, he decided to take a double-dip. He knew the Fangs would try to steal them back. After all, he was married to a woman from Hong Kong and knew the importance of saving face. My guess is he insured the shipment for theft and then he had Ruddy here reach out to an old sailing buddy to make sure the chips did get stolen and the heist would be blamed on the Fangs. Your job was to make sure the chips were retrievable. That way Huntington could feed them back into his new plant's production line. The insurance policy pays off and he sells the chips. Twice is nice, right? How am I doing so far?"

Brix sneered. "You think you're so smart, but where's it gotten you now?"

Jack forged ahead, explaining it to himself more than anyone else. "Mai dug around after hearing about the chips from me and discovered the insurance policy. She threatened to expose Huntington if he didn't play nice in the divorce. That's when Huntington got greedier. His type can't help themselves. He went after a second double-dip. Keep the insurance payoff and keep from paying off the wife. He sent Ruddy to keep Mai quiet. Permanently."

Jack smiled. “It was a good play all right, except Huntington forgot one thing. There’s always a wild card.” He hooked his thumb at Brad.

Brix jabbed the gun. “Game’s over. You’re still a loser. Check out the wild card now.” He ordered Cutler to put Katie and Brad in the Mercedes. “When you’re done with that, put a gun on these two assholes.”

“With pleasure,” Cutler said.

“Let Katie and Brad go,” Jack said. “You don’t need them anymore.”

“I’m big on insurance,” Brix said with a laugh. He turned to the winch monkeys who had loaded the container and closed its rear doors. “Get it out of here.”

They got in the cab and drove into the alley. Cutler finished shoving Katie and Brad into the backseat of the Mercedes and rejoined Brix, training a black automatic with walnut grips on Jack and Hark.

Brix flashed his jack-o’-lantern grin. “Payback’s a bitch, huh, McCoul?” He started for the Mercedes, calling to Cutler as casually as ordering a drink, “Make sure to shoot them in the head.” And then he got in the car with Katie and Brad and drove away.

The sunburned sailor flapped his bushy eyebrows and grinned. “Who wants to go first?”

Jack returned the grin. “Do you know why I call you Ruddy?”

Cutler pulled the hammer back. “I told you, don’t call me that.”

“It’s because you’re so ruddy blind. So’s Brix. So’s Huntington. You all never saw the double switch I just pulled. The container your winch monkeys drove off with? The boxes of chips are only two rows deep. The rest are filled with stolen laptops.”

“You’re lying. No way you’d risk your wife’s life.”

“I had no choice. It was the only way to sell it to a guy like

Brix. The truck's already been reported to the cops. Hark and I unloaded the chips by the time you got here. They're stacked in the next room."

"Bullshit," Cutler said, his face turning a bright crimson "You're only saying that to get me to look."

Jack held Cutler's stare. "No need to now. Like I said, you're not only dumb, you're ruddy blind, don't you know?"

Hark cleared the Beretta fast for a man his size and couldn't miss hitting a bull's-eye that red. He put one dead center.

33

Jack had been in the life long enough to know crims stuck to a pattern. Instead of trying to fight traffic all the way across the city, he bulleted the Prius straight for Pier 22½. He speed-dialed Terry Dolan as he steered.

"Huntington's the murderer," Jack shouted while whipping around a muni bus and narrowly avoiding a head-on with an oncoming delivery van. "It wasn't his arm that broke Mai's neck, but he ordered it done." He gave the detective the CliffsNotes version of the murder and insurance scam.

"Where's the guy who did the actual killing?" Terry asked.

Jack hesitated. He could see the fifty-yard line at Candlestick Park at two in the morning and the silhouette of a lowrider parked in the distance. "Don't worry about him. Arrest Huntington while he's delivering the keynote at the gamer convention. He's your headline. Three other witnesses can put him away. Two are in a carry container truck filled with stolen laptops. Check your e-mail. I sent you the link to an app. There's a transponder on the back of the TEU with a built-in LoJack that will lead you straight to them."

"You said three witnesses," Terry said carefully.

"I'm going to send him to you special delivery."

"What about Katie? Is she safe?"

Jack took a breath. Brix keeping her hadn't been part of the play, but there was only one shuffle of the cards remaining and he didn't trust anybody else to make it. "You concentrate on nailing Huntington," he said. "Leave Katie to me."

Jack clicked off the phone. He ran a red light on Embarcadero and then yanked a hard left. A trolley heading downtown nearly T-boned him. Tires screeched and bumpers clanked as he wove in and out of traffic. He swerved straight into the open bay of the fire station and slammed on the brakes the same time he hit the horn.

Marquis Williams came thundering out of his office, his unhooked yellow suspenders flapping below his thick waist. "What kind of crazy we got going on in here?"

"I need your help," Jack said as he jumped out of the Prius. "There's an emergency at the Franciscan Yacht Club. We got to get there fast."

The big fire fighter didn't ask what or why. He just yanked the cord to an old-fashioned brass bell and a half-dozen of San Francisco's finest came sliding down a pole from the bunkhouse above. They grabbed long black jackets and helmets that were hanging from a row of hooks and beelined straight for the *Phoenix*.

Jack chased Marquis to the wheelhouse. The skipper had the big Detroit diesels roaring to life with a push of a button. Black clouds belched from the exhaust stack and the hull shuddered. Someone threw the mooring lines as Marquis spun the oak wheel and cut a course toward the Golden Gate.

"What's going down?" he finally asked.

"It's Katie," Jack said, riding standing up, gripping the edge of the chart table for balance. "A guy who should never have been let out of the pen grabbed her and her brother. He's going to set sail and drop them in the deep blue."

"How do you know they're at the Franciscan?"

"It's his M.O. He always goes for a joyride to celebrate. One of his gang worked on a yacht there. It's where he's been hiding Katie and her brother. She told me so when she said Brad lost his equilibrium. Punk gets seasick facing a bowl of soup."

"Katie's in danger?" Marquis's face tightened as he shot Jack a fierce look. "Why the hell didn't you say so?" And he slammed the twin chrome throttle levers forward and the *Phoenix* jumped, its bow rising on plane, its siren screaming.

They rounded North Beach so close the fireboat sent a wave smashing against the piers and barely missed colliding with an inbound ferry from Sausalito. The *Phoenix* churned past Aquatic Park and Fort Mason, leaving a four-foot-high wake. Sailboats jibed to get out of their way and a kiteboarder, unable to turn in time, was forced to tug on his strings and jump. He soared so close Jack could see his lips moving as he cried for his mother.

The entrance to the yacht harbor was coming up fast, but Marquis didn't throttle back. "Which boat is she on?"

Jack recalled the magazine cover photos of Sinclair Huntington at the helm of a fifty-eight-foot Beneteau sailboat. "That one," he shouted, pointing to a yacht leaving the marina. Huntington's portrait as a Jolly Roger billowed as the sailboat's mainsail filled with wind.

The Beneteau heeled over from the stiff breeze and its knife-edge hull sliced cleanly through the chop as Brix steered for open water. The broad-beam fireboat could not match its speed but Marquis had tricks of his own. He had piloted the *Phoenix* in every kind of weather San Francisco Bay could throw, be it smothering fog, gale force winds, or flood tides coming and ebb tides going. He aimed the fireboat's bow straight into the path of the sailboat and sounded the horn.

Brix spun the wheel and tried to jibe.

"Careful," Jack warned. "He's got a gun."

"So do I," Marquis said. He bellowed into the boat's squawk box. "Man the monitors. Aim at the sails and knock the wind out of them. If that hostile on deck points a weapon, blast his ass."

Fire fighters raced to the fore and aft monitors. The powerful water guns were capable of spaying bursts that could extinguish an inferno two hundred feet away. The gunners let loose and jets of white water arced through the air and battered the Beneteau.

"He's trying to raise the spinnaker," Jack said. "If he gets that up, we'll lose him for sure."

Marquis ordered his crew to take it out. They rotated the brass nozzles and fired. The pressurized blast tore the sail loose from its sheets. Brix hunched lower in the cockpit but with no crew to handle the luffing mainsail, the racing yacht started to slow.

Jack grabbed a bullhorn and ran onto deck. "Give it up. It's over."

Brix pointed his gun and fired. The bullets pinged off the bridge.

"Back at you." Marquis swore and swung the *Phoenix* broadside, shooting a wake that pounded the yacht's hull.

"Don't sink him," Jack yelled. "Katie's tied below deck. She'll drown."

A cloud of black exhaust screened a fire fighter who ran to the starboard side and threw a grappling hook at the sailboat. It missed and raked the hull, clawing its glossy finish. Jack remembered the fancy boathook Huntington boasted he used on remoras as the fire fighter tossed the hook again. This time it snagged the Beneteau's chrome railing.

Brix scrambled below once he realized he was hooked. When he returned he was pushing Katie in front of him with the barrel of the gun jammed against her neck. She was still gagged, her wrists zip tied in front.

"Cut that line and back off," Brix snarled. "I'm sailing out of here. You follow me, she's dead."

"Give it up," Jack said. "You never had the chips; I pulled a *Jamaican* on you. They're still in the warehouse. Huntington can't help you. The cops got him for murder. He's handcuffed in the backseat of a Crown Vic by now."

Brix sneered. "He'll be out within an hour. His kind never does time." He ground the gun barrel harder into Katie's neck. "Now back the fuck off."

"Captain said we should do what he says," a fire fighter whispered to Jack. "He's radioed the Coast Guard. They're mustering a cutter. They'll be able to track him wherever he goes, take him out with a sharpshooter if he doesn't surrender."

Jack glanced at the thick bank of fog rolling in. "We can't let him take Katie out of the bay. This has got to end right now." He shouted to Brix, "Okay, we'll untie. Don't hurt her."

"First smart move you made all day," Brix said as he hid behind Katie.

Jack locked eyes with her. "You'll be okay, babe. I promise. Practice your yoga poses, especially the *Virabhadrasana*." And then he winked.

Katie's green eyes sparkled back. And then, in a single motion, she threw her head forward, bent perpendicular at the waist, and kicked her left leg straight back. Her perfectly arched foot with its bright red toenails caught Brix square in the balls. In the same blur of movement she rotated like a figure skater performing a camel spin and knocked the gun from his grip while she speared her bound hands straight into Brix's chest.

Jack leaped across the gunwale and landed beside Katie

before the splash Brix made hitting the water had settled. He tugged off the gag and kissed her. "One of these days you're going to have to teach me that Warrior pose."

Katie smiled, her eyes growing soft and sexy. "I can think of some other positions we can try first."

34

Mark Twain said the coldest winter he ever spent was a summer in San Francisco. Carl Sandburg wrote a poem about fog that came in on little cat feet and sat silently on its haunches watching the harbor and city. Twain wasn't exaggerating, but Sandburg was talking about Chicago, because the fog in Jack's town? It roared in like a lion, riding on a big, roiling cold current that swept from Canada and ran all the way to Baja. If Jack caught it, along with a stiff wind, he could sail to Cabo without making a tack.

That's exactly what he was doing as he held the Beneteau on a southerly course. The postcard-perfect coastline whipped by: Big Sur, Santa Barbara, L.A. Right past San Diego and the border guards at Tijuana.

Hola and adios, muchachos. We don't need no stinkin' visas.

Jack and Katie took turns being captain and first mate, both at the helm and in the stateroom's big bed. They were lying there, the sails trimmed by autopilot, and Katie was asking what Hark wanted when he called on the yacht's satellite phone.

"He said to tell you he's going to cherry out the Prius for you," Jack said. "Give it a new spray job and paint a mural on the sides. Add some chrome here and there. It'll be waiting for you when we get back."

Katie smiled. "Hark's so sweet, but he had more to say than that. What else did he tell you?"

"Nothing important. Just filled me in on what went down after we left." Jack checked her skin closely for sunburn.

"I told you already. I put sunscreen there. What did Hark say about Terry?"

"That he arrested Sinclair Huntington right on Moscone's center stage, a TV crew in tow to capture the whole thing. A thousand camera phones uploaded it to YouTube. The gamer audience thought it was all part of some marketing gimmick for a new app. They kept sitting in their seats after Terry slapped on the handcuffs and hauled him off, thinking Sinclair would somehow magically reappear."

"I'm sure he was very surprised when Terry showed up," she said.

"Huntington never saw it coming. He was so full of himself he couldn't imagine getting caught. Best part is now he knows he let his ego beat him. That playing it straight and divorcing Mai would've been a lot cheaper price to pay than betting on an insurance scam and murder."

"It wasn't just his ego that beat him," Katie said. "You and Hark did."

"And you too." Jack started examining her for more signs of sunburn.

Katie slapped his shoulder playfully. "What did Hark say about Terry? I bet the TV cameras made him look like one of those hunky actors who play cops in the movies."

Jack blew out some air. "Come on, babe, it's not like Hark and I sit around discussing what another guy looks like, especially a cop like Terry. He doesn't know what to put on first, his Jockey shorts or his badge."

"You like him," Katie said.

"You're crazy," he replied.

"Sure you do. Terry and you have been playing cops and robbers since you were five years old. You never outgrew it. Neither has he." She gave a pointed pause. "Of course, not that you'll ever play robber again. You're through with that for good, right? On your honor?"

Jack crossed his heart but he was thinking about Terry. The detective wouldn't have bought it for a second when Marquis Williams told him that the last time he saw Jack and Katie was when Jack pushed Brad overboard and told him to swim to the fireboat. No chance Terry would ever believe Huntington's yacht got lost in the fog while Jack and Katie were supposed to be following the *Phoenix* to port.

Jack wasn't worried about the detective coming after him anytime soon. Terry would have his hands full working confessions out of the twin winch monkeys and Brix while he built the case against Huntington. There was a promotion at stake. Besides, as soon as they rounded Cabo, Jack would head the Beneteau straight up the Sea of Cortez to Puerto Escondido. Bobby Ballena was living there. He brokered yachts and whatever else floated his way. He was the last person on earth to care about the name and home port written on a boat's stern. It's what marine paint was for, he'd say as he got the yacht ready to fence.

"I'm hungry," Jack said.

"For dinner?" Katie said.

"That too."

And she gave him another playful slap. They wrestled around for a while and then Jack went to the galley. Huntington's yacht was first class all the way, including his food stores and liquor cabinet. Jack started making margaritas using a $2,000 bottle of Barrique de Ponciano Porfidio.

He thought about his conversation with Hark. The rest of the play went down like Jack had planned. The chips stashed in the other part of the warehouse were reloaded into the TEU Brix had left behind. They were delivered to Jimmie and his dad in exchange for a fat finder's fee.

Jack fiddled with the marine band radio as he sliced limes and chilled the glasses. He found an NPR station. The top business story of the day was the beating Huntington's stock took when word got out about his arrest and the windfall a few day traders made shorting it.

Jack filled the sterling silver cocktail shaker with tequila, ice, and lime juice and started playing it like a maraca. A smile spread across his face as he shook, rattled, and rolled. When he had been sitting in the warehouse waiting for Brix to show, Jack had phoned Leonard and told him Big Angel wasn't going to let him in on the Series A funding, but he had a sure fire as a consolation prize. Call your broker, Jack told the computer whiz, and use your stock options as collateral and short all the Huntington stock you can get your hands on. Sell it by the end of the day and you'll make a bundle. Leonard said sure, and the 10 percent commission he agreed to pay Jack for the tip had already been wire transferred to his numbered account in the Caymans.

Jack switched to an oldies rock station. He twisted the rims of the crystal glasses in pink sea salt. Katie professed it was good for his heart. She glissaded into the galley, wearing a white and blue striped sailor shirt with a low-cut boat neck. Her hair cascaded onto the tops of her shoulders. She pressed against his back as he poured the margaritas.

"What's that you're humming?" Katie asked and started to nibble his ear.

"Just an old Bob Dylan tune," Jack said.

"Which one?"

"Idiot Wind."

As if on cue, the breeze picked up and the sails automatically adjusted, pushing the yacht faster toward Cabo.

Katie pressed harder into Jack's back, her arms tightening around his waist. "How does the refrain go?"

He sang it for her. *"I can't help it if I'm lucky."*

A NOTE FROM THE AUTHOR

Thank you so much for reading *A BOATLOAD*. I'd truly appreciate it if you would please leave a review on Amazon and Goodreads. Your feedback not only helps me become a better storyteller, but you help other readers by blazing a trail and leaving markers for them to follow as they search for new stories.

To leave a review, go to the *A BOATLOAD* product page on Amazon, click "customer reviews" next to the stars below the title, click the "Write a customer review" button, and share your thoughts with other readers.

To quote John Cheever, "I can't write without a reader. It's precisely like a kiss—you can't do it alone."

GET A FREE BOOK

Dwight Holing's genre-spanning work includes novels, short fiction, and nonfiction. His mystery and suspense thriller series include The Nick Drake Novels and The Jack McCoul Capers. The stories in his collections of literary short fiction have won awards, including the Arts & Letters Prize for Fiction. He has written and edited numerous nonfiction books on nature travel and conservation. He is married to a kick-ass environmental advocate; they have a daughter and son, and two dogs who'd rather swim than walk.

Sign up for his newsletter to get a free book and be the first to learn about his next novel as well as receive news about crime fiction and special deals.

Visit dwightholing.com/free-book. You can unsubscribe at any time.

ALSO BY DWIGHT HOLING

The Nick Drake Novels

The Sorrow Hand (Book 1)

The Pity Heart (Book 2)

The Shaming Eyes (Book 3)

The Whisper Soul (Book 4)

The Jack McCoul Capers

A Boatload (Book 1)

Bad Karma (Book 2)

Baby Blue (Book 3)

Shake City (Book 4)

Short Story Collections

California Works

Over Our Heads Under Our Feet

Made in the USA
Monee, IL
12 July 2020